CW01081775

Guyana Legends

KENSAL LIBRARY WITHDRAWN

3 0116 1750 6680

Guyana Legends

Folktales of the Indigenous Amerindians

Odeen Ishmael

Copyright © 2011 by Odeen Ishmael.

Library of Congress Control Number:		2011915203
ISBN:	Hardcover	978-1-4653-5669-7
	Softcover	978-1-4653-5668-0
	Ebook	978-1-4653-5670-3

All rights reserved. No part of this book may be reproduced or transmitted in any form or by any means, electronic or mechanical, including photocopying, recording, or by any information storage and retrieval system, without permission in writing from the copyright owner.

This is a work of fiction. Names, characters, places and incidents either are the product of the author's imagination or are used fictitiously, and any resemblance to any actual persons, living or dead, events, or locales is entirely coincidental.

This book was printed in the United States of America.

To order additional copies of this book, contact:
Xlibris Corporation
1-888-795-4274
www.Xlibris.com
Orders@Xlibris.com
103202

ACKNOWLEDGMENTS

I wish to acknowledge the dedication of my dear wife Evangeline for her tireless efforts in assisting with the editing of this book. My appreciation also is extended to my daughter Nadeeza and my niece Nalisa for their help in proofreading. I also thank my son Safraz, my nephews Sadiek, Rameez, and Fareek, as well as and my old friend Walter Gobin for their inputs of photography and other illustrations.

Many of the photographs illustrating this book were collected over a period of many years. I do not have a record of their source, but I take this opportunity to give acknowledgment to all who might have been involved in their original production.

Finally, I must express my deepest gratitude to all the persons of Amerindian ancestry who provided me with much of the original materials that form the basis of this publication. To them it is dedicated most sincerely.

CONTENTS

INTRODUCTION

The Amerindians of Guyana

Located on the northern shoulder of South America, the Republic of Guyana—a British colony up to 1966—is a relatively small country of 83,000 square miles (216,000 square kilometers) with a population of approximately 750,000. Roughly 85 percent of the people live on the narrow coastal plain bordering the Atlantic Ocean. This coastal plain, while being very low, is extremely rich in its fertile alluvial soils. The interior of the country is full of hills and mountains, interspersed with hundreds of rivers and creeks.

The remaining 15 percent of the population live in scattered villages in the interior, which is thickly forested, except for an area of savannah near the Brazilian border.

Among the people who live in the interior forests and savannah are the indigenous people—the Amerindians—comprising nearly 10 percent of the country's population. The name "Amerindians" is coined from two words—"American Indians"—to differentiate these people from the East Indians whose ancestors were brought from India by the British colonials during the nineteenth century to work as laborers and, later, to settle in the country. Currently, East Indians account for about 43 percent of the country's population. Other ethnicities include people of African origin (33 percent) and smaller groups of Chinese and Europeans (including Portuguese) with less than one percent each. A "Mixed" group accounts for about 13 percent of the inhabitants.

Amerindians were the original inhabitants of the country. Some historians claim that these indigenous people have been living in the country for over twelve thousand years. Traditionally, the Amerindians, who are

9

Mongoloid in physical appearance, have been forest dwellers, depending on hunting, fishing, and simple agriculture for food. Their agriculture has always been primitive, and their slash and burn method is generally still being applied up to this day—most likely because of the poor agricultural soils in the areas where they live.

Most of their villages are still located close to rivers and creeks, which—in addition to being routes on which they travel with canoes and motorboats—are important for fishing, bathing, and providing fresh water for domestic use.

When the Europeans came to the American continent at the end of the fifteenth century, there were an estimated 70,000 Amerindians in Guyana. However, after centuries of tribal warfare, migration to neighboring countries, plantation slavery, and culture shock from the clash with European civilization, their numbers were drastically reduced to 7,500 by 1891. Since then, there has been an upsurge in population growth, and today, the Amerindians number almost 80,000.

The Amerindian population is divided into nine tribal groups: Arawak, Arecuna, Akawaio, Carib, Makushi, Patamona, Wai-Wai, Wapishana, and Warrau. Tribal divisions are based on different languages and, to a lesser extent, on cultural traditions.

Traditionally, each tribe has occupied specific geographical areas. However, with internal migration, intermarriage between people of different tribes, the nearly universal use of the English language at the expense of tribal languages, and the almost complete conversion of Amerindians of all tribes to Christianity by missionaries, tribal divisions are becoming clouded in many areas. Complicating the situation is the adaptation to external culture forms, the accessibility to formal public primary and secondary education, and the general use and application of modern technology—including the use of airplanes and motorboats for traveling; guns for hunting; and the radio, television, and the Internet to receive and transmit information.

Also of importance is the creation by the Makushi, Akawaio, and Carib tribes of an indigenous religion known as *Hallelujah* which is heavily based on Christianity but incorporates elements of those tribes' traditional beliefs as well.

Significantly, most young people of all tribes, almost all of whom have received at least six years of formal education in schools, rarely communicate in the tribal languages or have totally forgotten them. However, some efforts are being made to revive and preserve these language forms through, *inter alia*, the compilation of dictionaries.

In addition, the Amerindians are more and more being absorbed into the wider Guyanese society. And they no longer have a primitive outlook. Traditional clothing of loincloths and beads is hardly ever worn because modern clothing is the trend. But while some have achieved relatively very high levels of modern education and are now teachers, nurses, civil servants, members of parliament, and ministers of the government, the interior areas where the Amerindians live still remain the least economically developed parts of the country.

It is also worthy to note that the Amerindians have adapted to the money economy and have moved away almost entirely from their traditional bartering system. In some areas, many of the able-bodied men work on the timber grants for several months of the year. During that time, the farms are tended generally by women and children. In the Rupununi savannahs near the Brazilian border, Amerindian men also are employed as *vaqueros* on the large cattle ranches. Others are small gold miners while some are seasonal *balata* "bleeders"—balata being the natural rubber formed from the sap of the *bulletwood* tree.

Even though their subsistence farms produce a variety of fruits, vegetables, and root crops, *cassava* remains the main produce and the chief item on the Amerindian diet. And while there are two main types of cassava (sweet cassava and bitter cassava), the Amerindians cultivate mainly the bitter variety, which has poisonous acids in the juice.

When the cassava is grated, squeezed in a basketwork tube known as a *matapee* to remove the cassava juice that contains the poisonous acids, then dried, sifted, roasted, fermented, and processed in many other ways, a variety of foods is produced, including cassava bread, *farine, casiri*, and *paiwarri*. In addition, *casareep*—a very dark preservative sauce—is made from the juice through a long boiling process to neutralize the acids.

The contribution of the Amerindians to Guyanese society is most noteworthy. For example, the preservative sauce *casareep* is used in making pepperpot, a very popular dish in Guyana that consists mainly of meat and hot peppers. This dish has become national and is highly popular among all ethnic and cultural groups in the country.

Some other significant contributions of the Amerindians are the making and use of the hammock, the identification and use of innumerable medicinally valuable indigenous plants, the manufacture and use of the drug *curare*, the domestication and "education" of the parrot (Amerindians first taught it to speak), and the naming of many of the country's rivers, mountains, flora, and fauna.

All these aspects of Amerindian culture and economic development are mentioned to give the reader some background behind the stories in this collection.

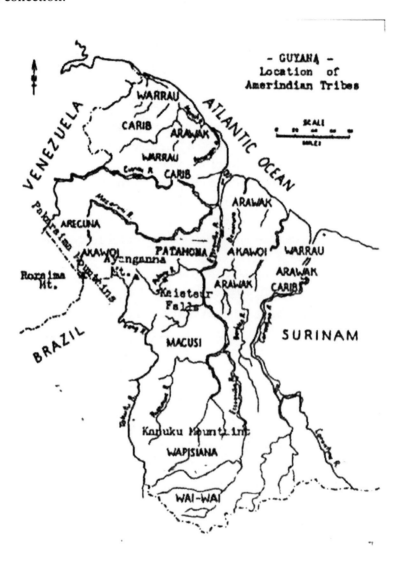

Map of Guyana showing the traditional areas
occupied by the Amerindian tribes

Woman using a matapee to extract cassava juice

Amerindian schoolchildren

This collection of folktales

While very little is known of Amerindian history in Guyana before the arrival of European settlers in the early seventeenth century, no written form of their languages existed until about seventy-five years ago. And much of the history is based on oral traditions, which are not quite clear because the periods when important events occurred are difficult to place. Still, native oral traditions are very rich in folk stories of the ancestral heroes and heroines of the Amerindian people.

Some of these folk stories have varying versions among the nine different language groups—or tribes—that comprise the Amerindian population of Guyana. Such a difference is illustrated in this book, which presents two different tales of how fire was acquired and various versions of the legend of two immortal folk heroes: the bothers Makonaima and Pia.

This present collection of Amerindian legends was compiled over a lengthy period of many years during which I listened to and collected versions of these tales from elderly Amerindians in various regions of Guyana and, more recently, from Amerindian residents of the Delta Amacuro region of Venezuela, on the frontier with Guyana.

Significantly, most of these legends were also summarized since the late nineteenth century by a succession of writers, including Everard F. im Thurn, W. H. Brett, Walter Roth, and Leonard Lambert. But it is significant to note that the versions—which by no means were original—that were related by those writers of the nineteenth and early-twentieth centuries have undergone some changes with the passing years, and new characters have been added to them.

Since Amerindians of the North-West District of Guyana are ethnologically and culturally related to those in the eastern regions of Venezuela, particularly the Delta Amacuro region, it is noteworthy that the myths and legends of those Venezuelan Amerindians bear close similarities to those of their Guyanese counterparts. Interestingly, the Guajiro people—Amerindians of Arawak background living in north-west Venezuela near to Lake Maracaibo—also have some folktales that closely resemble those of their "relatives" living in the North-West District of Guyana and the Delta Amacuro region of Venezuela. For further information, the writings of Venezuelan researchers Cesaréo de Armellada, Maria Manuela de Cora, and Michel Perrin are recommended.

It is essential to note too that an important character in Amerindian legend is "Tiger." While there are a number of tigers in the stories—and generally they are all villains—these animals, however, are not part of the fauna in Guyana or the entire American continent. What is generally referred to as a tiger is the large spotted jaguar. And the "black tiger" mentioned in one of the stories in this book is the large South American puma.

My earlier book—*Amerindian Legends of Guyana*, which was published in 1995—contains twenty of the folktales in this current collection for which they have been revised and, in some cases, retitled. Among the thirty other stories are those of two clever tricksters in Amerindian folklore: the lazy but sly Konehu and the wily rabbit Koneso.

I do hope that readers find these folktales of the original inhabitants of Guyana informative in the anthropological sense, in addition to being interesting and entertaining at the same time.

Odeen Ishmael
Guyana, 2011

~ 1 ~

How the First People Arrived on Earth

A long, long time ago, there were no human beings on Earth. However, at that time, a group of people known as the Warraus lived in Skyland, but they had no idea that Earth existed.

Up in Skyland, there lived among these people a famous and skilful hunter: Okonorote. Each time Okonorote set out to hunt, he would always return home with something. For instance, if he went after a bush-hog or a bird, he never gave up the chase until he caught the animal. At times, he would chase his prey mercilessly for days until he could shoot it down with his bow and arrow.

As Okonorote hunted in the forest one day, he saw a fat wild turkey, and he swore he would not rest until he captured it. Soon he discovered that the turkey was so agile that it led him on a tiresome chase for several days. Deeper and deeper into the dense, humid forest, the turkey led Okonorote. But in the end, he managed to hit the bird with his sharp arrow. It instantly fell and disappeared into a deep pit on the forest floor.

Still, Okonorote did not give up. He was determined, as ever before, to have that turkey. He thought that he had not chased the bird for all those days only to leave it in the hole. So he moved closer and knelt beside the hole to see where the turkey landed. Peeping down the hole, Okonorote was awestruck.

Way down below, he strained his eyes as he gazed upon a strange land where many animals walked about idly. They all seemed very small to him, although some were taller than others. Okonorote gazed at the scene for quite some time. Then he hurried home.

His tribesmen, as they usually did after his arrival in the village from each hunting expedition, gathered to greet him and examine his catch for the day.

But this time, Okonorote surprised them all. He came home empty-handed.

"Okonorote, where's the animal you were hunting?" an old man asked.

"This is the first time you ever came home empty-handed!" another man observed.

Okonorote looked at them and then explained, "My friends, it's true I have returned empty-handed for the first time, but I followed a wild turkey for many days. When I finally shot it, it fell into a deep hole in the forest floor. I looked into the hole to find the turkey but saw a strange land at the bottom where many animals grazed. I saw no human beings there."

"Take us to this hole," a young man urged.

"Come, let us go," Okonorote replied.

Okonorote, followed by all the men and older boys of his village, returned to the hole deep in the forest.

"Look into the hole and tell me if I haven't spoken the truth," he said.

One by one they looked, and it was just as Okonorote had reported—hundreds of animals lived on the strange land below.

And since all the men of the village were hunters, their mouths watered at the sight of all those animals. They now yearned to get down there so they could have meat all year round. But one big problem existed: they did not know how to reach that land.

With this in mind, the men suggested different ideas, but Okonorote solved the problem. "Let's weave a long rope from all these bushes growing here. We can tie one end to that tree trunk, and we'll drop the rest down the hole. I'll then climb down the rope to the land below. When I'm ready to come up, I'll tug the rope twice. You can then haul me up."

The men wasted no time. Quickly they worked together and wove a long rope, which they dropped down into the hole. Then Okonorote, armed with his bow and arrow, climbed down swiftly. After a while, he set foot on the strange, distant land.

The first thing Okonorote did was to look for the turkey, which he found lying on some soft grass. As he examined his surroundings, he was amazed at the richness of the land and at the large number of animals that lived there. Seeing a large deer grazing nearby, he shot it and set it beside the turkey. That was certainly the first deer he ever saw in his life, for Skyland had no such animal.

As Okonorote prepared for his journey back to Skyland, he tied the deer and turkey to the rope. Then he held on to it firmly and tugged twice. Far above, his friends felt the tugging, and they eagerly pulled him up.

Later that day, they butchered the deer and shared it among all the families in the village. The meat was so tasty that everyone, including the women and children, felt they too should go to the strange land to hunt more deer.

The next morning, all the villagers—men, women, and children—began to climb down the rope to the new and exciting land below.

Then disaster struck.

A very stout woman, who managed to get only halfway through the hole, got stuck. Those who had already arrived in the new land tugged desperately on the rope to free her. Still, she remained stuck. Meanwhile, those in Skyland climbed down into the hole to pull the woman up; but even so, she remained stuck. As darkness closed in, everyone grew tired and eventually gave up.

And ever since that day, the Warraus who had arrived in the new land—which was really the Earth—were forced to remain there. Meanwhile, the people in Skyland could not descend either, because the poor stout woman blocked the hole linking Earth and Skyland.

To this day, she still remains in the hole. At times, in loneliness, she cries bitterly; and as she does so, her tears fall to the Earth as rain.

The deer

The turkey

~ 2 ~

The Wonderful Tree

A long, long time ago, the great forest spirit Tamosi created a special tree, which he placed in the forest. But though the tree looked similar to others, it produced almost all the different useful fruits and vegetables in the world. The tree was left there purposely by Tamosi for people or animals to discover and make use of its produce.

It was shortly after people began living on Earth that Maipuri, the tapir, while roaming in the forest one day, accidentally bumped into the strange tree. He was absolutely astonished, for he had never, in his life, seen so many different kinds of fruits and vegetables hanging from the same tree. In fact, it was the first time he had seen some of those fruits and vegetables.

"This tree will feed me for the rest of my life," Maipuri contemplated.

After he ate as much fruits and vegetables as he could, he went back to the village at the edge of the forest where he lived with other animals among the people.

During that period, a dreadful famine enveloped the entire land. Very little food was available, not only for people but for animals as well. Even in the rivers and creeks, fishes became scarce. Everyone was virtually starving.

But the selfish Maipuri decided not to tell anyone of the wonderful magical tree he discovered. With the food shortage throughout the entire land, he would be forced to share the fruits and vegetables with everyone. But he had no intention whatsoever to do so.

"If I tell the animals and human beings of this tree, I won't have enough to eat, and the food will finish way too quickly," he reasoned.

So every day onward, Maipuri went, all alone, deep into the forest to the wonderful tree. And after stuffing himself like a glutton, he returned to the village in the evenings. With the amount of food he was eating, he soon became excessively plump.

The people in the village noticed that Maipuri was getting fatter and fatter.

"Where are you getting food, Maipuri?" they asked. "You're being very selfish if you have food and keep it all to yourself."

"Just because I'm getting fat doesn't mean I've found food," he replied. He deliberately ignored the villagers and other animals and went home to sleep.

But Maipuri's actions soon aroused the curiosity of the villagers.

"Let's send some men to follow him when he goes into the forest in the morning," some villagers suggested. "If the men follow him, they'll be able to see where he gets his food and bring some back for us."

Early the next morning, five young men set out secretly behind the tapir. But the sly Maipuri saw them coming and slipped away among some thorn bushes.

The thorns did no harm to the tapir because of his tough skin, but the men were forced to give up their chase. They returned disappointedly to the village and told everyone about Maipuri's escape.

"Now we know he's found food in the forest," one of the young men said. "Otherwise, he wouldn't have slipped away from us. We have to follow him secretly and find the source of his food."

The villagers came up with other means of following the tapir. "Let's send Woodpecker to trace him," one old man suggested. "Woodpecker will fly in the air, and Maipuri won't suspect him."

Everyone thought that was a brilliant idea and immediately agreed. The next day, Woodpecker followed the tapir quietly into the forest. But Woodpecker could not resist tapping on trees along the route. Soon, Maipuri heard the steady tapping and realized that Woodpecker was following close behind.

"So they've sent Woodpecker to follow me," he chuckled. "I know how to fool him."

Suddenly, Maipuri darted from the track into the thick bushes to an area with many dead trees. There were countless worm holes on the tree trunks. Hiding under the nearby bushes, Maipuri watched as Woodpecker flew toward the trees.

The bird surely could not resist the worms and began tapping away vigorously. Maipuri knew that Woodpecker would not leave the area until he was finished checking all the holes.

Maipuri then smiled to himself and moved away quietly to the magic tree where he had a lavish meal. In the evening, as darkness slowly crept upon the land, Maipuri journeyed home and could still hear Woodpecker tapping at the dead trees.

It was late that night when Woodpecker returned to the village and reported his failed mission to the villagers.

Another lengthy discussion started, and the villagers decided to send Rat, this time, to follow Maipuri. The villagers all felt that Rat was the perfect choice. He was small and moved about quietly.

The next day, Rat followed Maipuri to the magic tree. As Rat approached the tree, he saw Maipuri lying under the tree and chewing a mouthful of cassava.

"So this is where you get your food," Rat said. "You're very selfish and greedy. Don't you want others to enjoy the fruits the same way you do?"

"Look, Brother Rat," replied Maipuri, "If I show this tree to everyone, in no time all the fruits will be eaten. Why don't we keep this secret together, then only the two of us will enjoy these tasty fruits?"

Rat, being a selfish animal himself, readily agreed to Maipuri's suggestion. He sat beside the tapir and stuffed himself with as much corn he could eat for a week.

Late that evening, he returned to the village. "I'm sorry, but Maipuri was too clever for me," he told the villagers. "I lost his track in the forest and, after trying for hours to find it, I gave up and decided to come home."

Every day, the villagers and other animals watched Maipuri growing fatter and fatter. However, no one ever suspected Rat. He was clever enough to slip away to the tree at nights to eat.

But one morning, Rat overslept. He had returned home just before daybreak and was awfully tired. He was so tired that he even fell asleep on his doorstep and snored with his mouth wide open.

Sigu, the old fisherman who was passing by that morning, saw some grains of corn stuck to Rat's teeth! At once, Sigu alerted the villagers who came and angrily shook Rat awake.

"You were fooling us!" they shouted. "Where did you get the grains in your mouth?"

"I won't tell you!" Rat yelled back.

"If you don't tell us, we'll feed you to Cat," Sigu warned.

Rat trembled with fear, for he was terribly afraid of Cat. He quickly revealed the secret. Upon hearing such good news, the people forced him to lead them to the magic tree deep in the forest.

And what a wonderful tree it was! On its branches hung plantains, bananas, cassava, yams, corn, papayas, and fruits and vegetables of all kinds.

The people and animals that came ate like gluttons. And when they could eat no more, they went to sleep under the tree's shady branches. When they awoke, they were surprised to see a strange old man standing nearby.

"Who are you?" they asked.

"I am Tamosi, the forest spirit," he replied. "I planted this tree."

"We're sorry we ate without your permission," Sigu apologized.

"Don't be sorry," the forest spirit replied. "I planted this tree so all humans and animals could have fruits when they need them, but I certainly don't want anyone to be selfish like Maipuri and Rat. Everyone must learn to share. So I want you to cut down the tree and divide the branches equally. Then go home and plant the branches in your own plots. In this way, you will have all the fruits and vegetables you need."

For many weeks thereafter, the people of the village cut away at the thick tree trunk with their stone axes. Eventually, the tree fell. They took away the branches and planted them in their respective gardens.

As time went by, people began reaping cassava, sweet potatoes, corn, bananas, papayas, and many other fruits and vegetables. Indeed, it was from those very branches that so many plants bearing different fruits and vegetables began to grow all over the world.

And as for the selfish Maipuri and Rat, they were so ashamed of themselves that they moved away into the forest and lived alone.

Maipuri, the tapir

~ 3 ~

The Great Flood

A few months after the magic tree was cut down, Sigu, the old man who had made the final chop of the trunk, returned to the spot where the tree once stood. To his surprise, he found the stump was hollow down the middle. Inside the stump, he also discovered water with many different kinds of young fishes swimming about.

"Why are all these little fishes here?" he wondered.

He thought for a moment and said, "I know what I'll do. I'll put the fishes in the streams and rivers around here."

So for months, Sigu traveled patiently throughout the land to distribute the little fishes in the various rivers and streams. After completing this task, he went back to the tree trunk for a final look.

To his surprise, he found the water overflowing steadily onto the ground. Sigu swiftly made a *warrampa*—a basket woven from reeds—and covered the stump with it. Instantly the hole was sealed, forcing the water to remain inside the tree trunk.

Around that same time, in a tiny village in another part of the forest, Iwarrika, the monkey, was caught stealing corn from a farm. He was taken before the village elders to be put on trial for his misdeed.

"For stealing corn, you must fetch water with a basket from the river and fill the empty duck pond," the chief elder told him.

For months, Iwarrika fetched water with the reed basket to fill the pond, but his efforts were in vain. In spite of this, he made his many trips to the river more interesting by following different tracks through the forest.

One day as he moved through one of these tracks, he encountered the tree trunk covered with the warrampa. Iwarrika stopped and was puzzled as to why an upside-down warrampa was on the tree stump.

"I'm sure that someone must have hidden a lot of fruits under it," he reasoned.

So he crept closer and closer and, with one swift movement, snatched away the warrampa. Instead of discovering fruits, a heavy stream of water gushed out from the hollow tree trunk.

Iwarrika screamed for help, but no one heard his little voice. The water kept flowing with such mighty speed that it overtook him. Sadly, he was drowned.

And soon, the forest floor was also covered with water. But it kept rising so rapidly that not long after, even the villages were covered.

There was great panic, especially in Sigu's village. Some people ran away while others headed for the distant mountains. But most of them were overtaken by the water and drowned.

But Sigu did not panic. He swiftly gathered all the animals that could not swim and locked them in a cave with a narrow entrance. After leaving the animals with a thin thorn, he sealed the entrance from outside with beeswax.

"Every day, bore a tiny hole through the wax with the thorn," Sigu told them. "Then look through the hole. You will be able to check the water level."

With that, Sigu climbed the tallest *kookrit* palm and made himself comfortable among the top branches. All the birds and the beasts that could climb also went up the palm tree with him. The flood eventually reached the level of the branches and then, luckily, it stopped rising.

For many weeks thereafter, Sigu lived in the palm tree with the birds and beasts. Every morning, he cautiously dropped a kookrit seed to check the water level. As time slowly passed by, the animals grew impatient. The red howling monkey began to roar so loudly that his throat swelled. And ever since, howling monkeys have swollen throats.

When the flood eventually receded and land could be seen once again, Sigu and the animals decided it was time to climb down. Without hesitation, Sigu rushed to the cave and released the animals locked inside.

But Sigu and his animal friends were not the only survivors. Marerawara and his family also survived the awful flood.

Before the flood, Marerawara lived near the Cuyuni River. He was very kindhearted and never turned away anyone who went to his house for cassava or sweet potatoes.

The same could not be said of the others living in his village. They were oftentimes quarrelsome. They even stole other people's crops at night.

One night, Marerawara had a strange dream in which he saw his village covered with water. He regarded his dream as an omen and told people of his fears.

"The whole land will be flooded," he said. "We must prepare for it."

But they laughed at him in scorn and disbelief.

"You're a dreamer! Why don't you leave us alone?" they mocked him.

In spite of this, Marerawara believed strongly in his dream. So he tied a strong bush rope to his big canoe, anchoring it to a tall tree near his home. He put his wife, his four children, and several of the animals he reared into the canoe. For food, he stocked dried meat and many kinds of fruits. Lastly, he climbed in.

As soon as he was finished with his preparations, the flood waters that covered Sigu's village reached Marerawara's village. Swiftly the flood waters rose, and the canoe rose with it as well. In no time, all the other villagers were drowned.

After many weeks when the water subsided, Marerawara's canoe finally touched ground and he, his wife, his four children, and his livestock climbed out anxiously. They soon began their task of building their home all over again.

Amerindian basket

~ 4 ~

Why Alligator Hates Other Animals

When the great flood ended, all the birds and other animals that were with Sigu on the kookrit palm climbed down to solid land. Soon, they were joined by those who had been locked up in the cave.

Of all the animals, the trumpet bird was in the greatest hurry. As soon as his feet touched ground, he at once rushed off into the forest in search of food. Indeed, he was unbearably hungry. Not mindful of where he was stepping, he accidentally landed on top of a ball of red ants, which had floated in the flood.

And since the ants were just as hungry as the trumpet bird, they clung ravenously to his meaty legs. In a wink, the bird's legs were reduced to a thin bony shape. And so, to this day, trumpet birds possess thin bony legs.

Sigu was also hungry, and so he immediately began to prepare a meal. Surrounded by a group of animals near to a small stream, he rubbed two pieces of dry sticks together to start a fire. Shortly after a spark flew off the wood, and the turkey, believing it was a firefly, flew up and swallowed it. Of course, it burned his throat. So in an effort to spit it out quickly, he made a strange sound: *gobble-gobble*. And as the heat from the spark penetrated the turkey's delicate throat, it formed big red lumps. Even to this day, all turkeys make that same *gobble-gobble* sound, and they still bear those red lumps under their throats.

But Sigu did not see the turkey swallow his spark. So he looked around for it but could not find it anywhere. He then turned to the other animals around him and asked, "Who stole the spark?"

No one knew that turkey swallowed it, so they all pointed to the alligator basking in the stream and shouted, "Alligator stole the spark!"

Sigu was convinced and became very angry. He jumped into the stream, grabbed the innocent Alligator, and tore out his tongue; but he never found the spark.

From that day onward, Alligator hated all other animals for the lie they told against him. He still has a small tongue, and he attacks the other animals whenever they come near.

The trumpet bird

~ 5 ~

The Caiman's Fire

Long, long ago, people ate their food raw because they possessed no fire. Only the fearsome caiman possessed fire at that time. Throughout the day, he hunted in the creeks and rivers and, in the evening, would return to his home in a cave near the riverbank. There he used the fire to cook his meal, which exuded a wonderful aroma that filled the air all around.

All the people and the animals living in the vicinity smelled this enticing aroma of the caiman's roasted meat and wished they could have a taste of it. The caiman became very powerful because he alone had cooked food, they reasoned.

Looking on from outside the cave, everyone could see the caiman cooking his food. He kept a ball of fire in his mouth, and when he opened it, the flame rushed out and lit a pile of dried sticks he had collected. Over this fire, the caiman roasted the wild meat he had set aside for his dinner. And after enjoying his meal, he would put out the fire, but he made sure he always kept a ball of flame in his mouth. When he closed his huge mouth, the fire could not be seen; but it remained inside, guarded by his powerful teeth and jaws.

Witnessing how the fire could spice up a meal and in dire need of having their food roasted as well, the people in the area came up with a plan.

"Let us all put our meat outside the caiman's cave and beg him to roast it with his fire," the chief suggested. "We should also tell him to take some for his service. Maybe that will encourage him."

This suggestion won acceptance, and the chief went to the caiman's cave to explain this proposal. Readily, the caiman agreed since it surely would save him much time from hunting for fish and wild meat.

And so, every day, the people delivered their wild meat at the mouth of the caiman's cave to be cooked. The caiman breathed his fire on it, and the roasted meat soon gave off a delectable aroma that tickled the taste buds of everyone in the vicinity. But every time they went to collect their roasted meat, they discovered that the caiman had taken a very large portion for himself. Despite this, they felt satisfied that, at least, they were having the opportunity to enjoy cooked food for themselves.

This arrangement with the caiman went on for quite some time, but eventually, everyone wanted some of the fire for himself and wondered how to get it from the caiman. What the people did was to check to see if he left any of it carelessly about so they could steal it for themselves. They watched as he left his cave in the morning as he set out to hunt. As usual, he caught fish and killed wild animals and took them back to his cave where he opened his mouth, set fire to his pile of sticks, and roasted everything before enjoying his meal. Then he made certain he closed his mouth as he slept so no one could steal the fire.

One day a boy, while hunting with his father in the forest, got separated from him and arrived, by chance, at the mouth of the caiman's cave. He peeped in and saw the beast sound asleep. Fully aware he was at the home of the "owner of fire," he became terrified, wondering if the caiman would suddenly wake up and see him. Despite his fear, he looked quickly about for any cooked food or a piece of burning stick, but he saw nothing except a burnt leaf near the mouth of the cave. Grabbing the burnt leaf, he hurried home to await his father.

When his father retuned home, he held up the leaf to his father.

"Father, I found this burnt leaf," he told him.

"Where did you find it?" his father asked in amazement.

"Near the mouth of the caiman's cave," the boy answered.

"Was the caiman there?" the father questioned. "Did you see any fire?"

"The caiman was sleeping," explained the boy. "His mouth was closed, so I could not see the fire."

"How can we ever manage to steal the caiman's fire?" the father mumbled.

"I think we should try to make him open his mouth so that someone can snatch it out," the boy suggested.

His father thought about what the boy suggested and, shortly after, came up with a plan.

The next day, after discussing his idea with his friend the hummingbird, he invited all the people and the animals in the area to a big party in his yard. He also invited the caiman who never missed an occasion when there was much to eat and drink.

Meanwhile, the host had told all the other guests in advance that when the caiman arrived at the party everyone should make jokes and do tricks that would make everybody laugh.

So when the caiman arrived, everyone took turns to crack jokes and do funny antics; and soon, the crowd was roaring with laughter. But the caiman did not laugh at all. He kept his big mouth tightly shut.

All the animals showed off their skills, and while everyone laughed and was having fun, the caiman did not even break a smile.

The birds did magnificent swoops in the air and brought expressions of "oohs" and "aahs" from the guests, but the caiman remained as glum as ever.

Finally, the green-tailed *jacamar* began a very funny dance. As the caiman looked on, he suddenly gave out a loud chuckle and burst out in loud laughter. Immediately, flames spurted from his mouth. All of a sudden, the hummingbird—as swift as ever—flew into the caiman's mouth, grabbed the ball of fire in his beak, flew away with it, and dropped it on a pile of dry wood. In no time, a great fire sprang up, and there was a mad rush to collect pieces of the burning wood.

As soon as the fire was stolen from the caiman's mouth, his tongue instantly shrank and became very small. Totally ashamed that he had now lost his control over fire, he rushed away from the party and hid himself in his cave. Soon after, knowing he no longer had any control over the people and animals around him, he abandoned his cave and took up residence in the depths of the river.

The caiman

The jacamar

~ 6 ~

The Boy Who Stole Fire

Long, long ago, people had no fire; so they ate all their vegetables, roots, and wild fruits raw. They also ate raw meat, but to preserve any extra quantity, they placed the surplus amount in the sun to dry.

And just like many wild animals, the first people lived in hollow tree trunks or caves. Later on, some built huts for their homes; but all of them lived without any warmth, especially on cold nights since they had no fire. During those chilly nights, there was no light either, and families huddled together for warmth and protection and from the fear of darkness.

The only one who possessed fire at that time was old Malewa, the mountain spirit who, in the form of an old man, lived in a cave on a mountainside far away from the villages. In his cave, he kept the fire in pieces of burning rock, and he gave specific instructions that no human or other living creature must ever come near to where he lived.

Malewa remained in his cave most of the time and kept himself warm by standing close to those burning rocks. He vowed to keep the fire only for himself and not let the people have any since he felt they would use it inappropriately. He feared, too, that they would use it to burn the forest and its living creatures, thus bringing disasters to the land. And even though he was so secretive about his fire, the people in the land knew he had it and yearned for that day when they could have some of their own for warmth and light.

One rainy day, as Malewa was warming his body near the fire, Junu, a fourteen-year-old boy, appeared at the mouth of his cave. He was wet and shivering with cold, and he had a small bag hanging from his shoulder. As soon as Malewa spotted the boy, he flew into a terrible rage, for no one could enter his cave without permission.

"What are you doing here?" he screamed in anger. "Don't you know that no one is allowed to come here? Have you come to disturb me?"

But Junu pleaded, "No, my honorable grandfather. I am wet and cold, and I have come to your place to warm my body."

However, the enraged Malewa, showing no pity whatsoever, replied, "You are rude to come here demanding warmth from my fire."

"I beg you to help me," Junu cried. "I meant no offence, but please allow me to warm myself for I am cold in my skin and bones. I promise to leave as soon as I feel warm."

By this time, Junu had noticed how comfortable and warm Malewa looked near the blazing rocks, and he was determined to obtain some of the heat emanating from them. What Junu did next was to trick Malewa in order to convince him that he was extremely cold. So he willfully made his teeth chatter noisily and trembled excessively while he rubbed his hands together to generate warmth. Such extreme actions soon convinced Malewa that the boy was indeed extremely cold.

"All right," Malewa conceded. "Come and stand near to me, but as soon as you become warm, you must leave. And do not come back here."

So Junu quickly moved from the mouth of the cave and stood beside Malewa next to the burning rocks. But the mountain spirit kept a close eye on him because he did not trust him at all. Meanwhile, Junu rubbed his hands together as his body absorbed the heat from the glowing rocks. It was indeed a very pleasant feeling for the boy.

As Junu stared at the burning rocks, he knew he could not leave the cave without first getting a piece of the hot material. Junu kept up a conversation to distract Malewa, but the old man paid no attention to him and kept his eyes focused on the burning rocks.

Then, all of a sudden, there was a noise at the mouth of the cave. It was only a gust of wind, but Malewa spun around to take a quick look. In a flash, Junu seized this advantage and snatched two small glowing stones and hid them quickly in his bag. Then, with lightning speed, he fled from the cave and disappeared in the surrounding forest.

Malewa immediately knew he was tricked by Junu and robbed of some of his fiery rocks, so he ran out of the cave to capture and punish him.

Meanwhile, the boy found that his escape was becoming difficult. The heavy rain had made the land very slippery, and he experienced great difficulty in moving quickly over the slippery, muddy ground. As he tried to increase his pace, he saw his friend Kena, a young hunter his own age, emerging from the bushes nearby.

"Kena, I'm bogged down in the mud, and I can't run fast enough," Junu told him. "I stole two fire stones from Malewa's cave, and I am sure he is trying to catch me."

Upon hearing this, Kena became excited, for he, like everybody else, dearly wanted a piece of the fiery rock.

"Where are the fire stones?" he asked anxiously.

Junu removed one of the glowing pieces of rock from his bag.

"Here," he said. "Run away now and hide it."

Without any delay, Kena dropped the burning stone in his arrow bag and rushed away from the area. He ran until night set in, but as darkness enveloped the land, Malewa, without much difficulty, saw the glow of the burning stone in the distance. Unable to contain his anger, he immediately punished Kena by transforming him into a firefly now emitting a flickering light as he flew among the bushes.

In the meantime, Junu, who had taken a new path in his bid to escape, nearly bumped into Jimut, another of his friends.

"Why are you in such a hurry?" his friend asked.

"Malewa is chasing me because I stole his fire, which I am bringing for all the people," Junu explained.

Eagerly, Jimut asked, "Where is it? Show it to me."

With that, Junu removed the last piece of glowing rock from his bag and handed it to him.

"Run away and hide it from Malewa," he instructed.

With great speed, Jimut ran away with the burning stone in his bare hand. But the stone began to burn his hand, and in discomfort, he threw it into a thick clump of bushes where it remained hidden from view. Not even Malewa could see its glow in the darkness.

By this time, Junu had arrived home, and he quickly spread the news that he had escaped with some of Malewa's fire and had given two pieces of the fiery rocks to his friends to hide. But no one could find Kena, while Jimut explained that he had thrown the piece given to him in a clump of bushes. Since he could not identify the particular clump, all the people began to search for the fiery stone. But with all their effort, no one could find it.

Then one day, a little girl came to the clump of *hima-hera*, broke two pieces of its dry roots sticking out from the ground, and playfully rubbed them together near to a pile of dried grass. All of a sudden, the dried grass began to smoke, and a fire broke out into a blaze. This was exactly the same clump of bushes into which Kena had thrown the fire stone, and it was apparent that the ignition quality of the hot stones was absorbed by the roots and stems of the hima-hera plant. Ever since that day, people would rub two pieces of hima-hera twigs against each other to create a fire.

And that was how the people came to possess fire, which they used for warmth and light during the night and, best of all, for cooking their food.

As for Malewa, he soon knew that he no longer possessed the secret of fire; so he reverted to his spirit form, and no one ever saw him again.

Malewa's cave

~ 7 ~

The First Carib

Deep in the forest, in the middle of a Warrau village, was a peaceful lake. From that lake, the Warraus obtained their drinking water and an abundant supply of fish all year round.

However, it was against the village rule to swim in the lake, and many children in the village questioned this rule. The elders explained, "A long time ago, the Great Spirit told our people to drink the water and catch the fish, but we were never to swim in the lake. Our grandparents and our parents obeyed that law, and you must obey it too. If you don't, bad things will happen to you."

That explanation satisfied most of the young people, and therefore, no one used the lake for anything else but fishing and collecting drinking water. Any swimming at all was done in the river that fed the lake. Because of this, peace prevailed upon the entire village, and everyone was happy.

But not far from the lake stood a little house in which eight persons lived. They were Koroma and Koroko, the father and mother; four brothers named Kororoma, Kororomana, Kororomatu, and Kororomatitu; and two sisters named Korobona and Korobonako.

Since the family lived ever so close to the lake, their parents warned the children repeatedly not to swim in the lake. However, the two girls became curious. One day they secretly decided to swim in the lake to find out what would happen.

Meanwhile, at the bottom of the lake lived the most powerful Water Spirit in the whole region. Many generations before, the magicians of the Warraus had to plant an old tree trunk possessing magic powers in the middle of the lake to keep the Water Spirit under control and protect the people from him. If anyone should touch that tree trunk, all its magic powers would disappear, and the Water Spirit would get out of control and harm the people. This was the reason no one was allowed to swim in the lake. However, all of this was unknown to all those who lived near the lake.

Anyway, early one morning, the curious sisters Korobona and Korobonako slipped quietly from the house before dawn and plunged into the cool, refreshing water.

"This is so beautiful!" Korobona said.

"Yes," replied Korobonako. "It's stupid for the old people to keep us from enjoying ourselves in the lake."

"Let's race to that old tree trunk," shouted Korobona as she swam quickly toward it.

Her sister followed closely behind.

Korobona reached the tree trunk first. She grabbed and shook it vigorously. At once, the spell controlling the Water Spirit was broken. Up jumped the Water Spirit in the form of a man to the surface of the lake near the tree trunk. Without hesitation, he snatched Korobona by her hair and swiftly pulled her down through the water to his home under the surface of the lake.

In disbelief, Korobonako watched as her sister was dragged away from her. In great terror, she swam back to the bank and hurried home to tell her parents and brothers what had happened.

Meanwhile, in the Water Spirit's home, Korobona became terribly afraid and expected to face death at any moment.

"If you become my wife, you'll be safe," the Water Spirit assured her. "One day, you can return to your people."

"What will happen if I refuse?" asked the frightened girl.

"You die immediately," the Water Spirit answered.

With no other option, she agreed to live with the Water Spirit and be his wife. As time passed, she gave birth to a son, but he was considerably strange. Even though he was beautifully formed, the lower part of his body from the waist down resembled a *camudi*!

A few weeks after the birth, the Water Spirit told Korobona, "You will now go back with our child to your home above the lake. If, at any time, you need my help, shake the tree trunk in the middle of the lake, and I will be there for you."

Korobona then swam to the surface with her strange child and set out toward her parents' home.

By this time, everyone in the village believed that Korobona had died. Thus her parents, brothers, and sister were extremely shocked when she walked through the door of their home with her half-human son. They were even more surprised to hear her strange story, and her parents quickly forgave her for breaking the village rule.

"At least the Water Spirit won't annoy us," her parents said. "He is now our son-in-law."

However, her brothers would not forgive her. "No, she must go away," they declared. "She has brought disgrace upon us for not obeying the law of our people."

But her parents insisted that she must live with them. They explained, "She is our daughter. Her child is our grandson."

Even though her brothers grumbled, they finally accepted their parents' decision but bluntly refused to speak to Korobona. Her sister Korobonako helped to care for the child though.

One night, the four brothers secretly planned to kill the child, but Korobona overheard their whispers. She at once suspected they were planning to harm her child, and after her brothers fell asleep, she slipped away from the house and hid her son in the forest.

Every day, she visited the secret hiding place to feed him. But her visits did not remain secret for long; for her brothers, one day, followed her to the location. Korobona had just finished feeding her baby and was playing with him on the grass under the tall trees when her brothers arrived. They immediately shot the baby with arrows and ran off.

Korobona quickly pulled out the arrows and treated her son's wounds with juices from plant leaves that grew around the hiding place. After a few months, the child recovered; and he soon grew up to be a huge half-man, half-snake.

At first, her brothers thought that they had killed the child; but after they saw Korobona still slipping away into the forest day after day, they realized that their plan had failed.

Again, they followed her into the forest, but this time they were astounded to see the size of her son. They swiftly hurried home and prepared many arrows and other weapons to kill him. When Korobona saw the vast amount of weapons, she knew her brothers must have followed her into the forest again and had discovered that her son was alive.

She felt that she must quickly warn her son of the impending danger. She slipped away quietly from the house and ran nonstop into the thick forest. However, her brothers were watching her closely. They grabbed their weapons and raced after her.

As her son crept out from his hiding place to greet her, the brothers showered him with piercing arrows. The arrows injured him so severely that he lay helpless on the ground.

The brothers then chopped him into little pieces as his mother stood by and wept.

"He is surely dead now!" they shouted, and ran off.

Korobona wept brokenheartedly over her son's mutilated remains for hours.

At last, she covered the pieces of his body with heaps of green leaves and walked slowly toward the lake. She plunged into the calm water and swam to the tree trunk. She grabbed and shook it firmly.

Immediately, her husband, the Water Spirit, appeared beside her.

"What is the matter, Korobona?" he asked.

"Our son is dead," she told him. "My brothers shot him with arrows. When he was helpless, they chopped him into little pieces. I want revenge."

"Go back to where the body lies," the Water Spirit instructed. "Keep watch over it, and soon, you shall have your revenge."

Korobona returned to the place where her son's body lay. She stared at the pile of leaves covering the body and cried bitterly all day.

As evening approached, the leaves began to shake steadily but gently. Then up popped a huge, handsome warrior, fully human. He held his bow and arrows, and he was dressed for battle.

He looked at Korobona and whispered, "My dear mother, you will have your revenge. My name is Carib. I'll drive away those who have tormented us."

Leaving her standing there, he rushed through the forest and attacked his uncles and all other Warraus who came to their aid. No one could match Carib's strength. In no time whatsoever, he killed his wicked uncles and drove the other Warraus before him.

Later, he returned to his mother. For a while, he lived happily with her, his aunt, and his grandparents on the bank of the peaceful lake. The most beautiful of the Warrau maidens became his wife; and his children became brave, strong warriors like himself.

In a relatively short time, a fierce Carib tribe grew up and lived on the bank of that lake. Later, when the Warraus tried to regain their homes and land that Carib originally seized, the fierce Carib tribe drove them to the muddy shores of the Atlantic Ocean and took full possession of their rich hunting grounds in the forest.

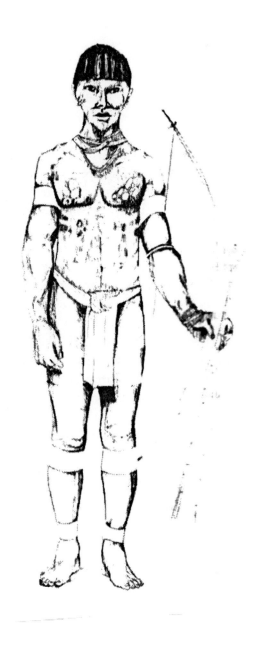

Sketch of a Carib warrior (a seventeenth-century depiction)

Warrau children in a canoe

~ 8 ~

The Marriage of Yar and Usidiu

Long, long ago, an old magician named Nahakaboni lived in the forest. He had a beautiful daughter, Usidiu, who was kind, pleasant, and hardworking. All the people and animals that lived in the forest loved her very much.

One day, while Usidiu was fetching water from the river, Yar, the Sun Prince, spotted her. At once, he fell madly in love and made a vow to marry her.

The next morning, the Yar went to Nahakaboni's home to ask for Usidiu to be his wife.

"Nahakaboni," he said, "My name is Yar, the Sun Prince. I saw your beautiful daughter by the river yesterday. If I don't marry her, I will surely die for I love her dearly."

Usidiu, who was eavesdropping in another room, peeked through a hole in the wall. She was amazed to see the tall, handsome Sun Prince, and she too immediately fell in love with him. Her only hope was that her father would agree to the Prince's request.

Nahakaboni, who loved his daughter dearly, felt that the person who wanted to marry her must be able to perform difficult tasks. So he said to Yar, "I will agree for the marriage, but on one condition. You must perform three difficult tasks. Only if you perform these tasks will you prove that you can care for my daughter."

"Oh, Nahakaboni," replied Yar, "I'm most willing to carry out your wishes."

"Well, here is your first task," said the old man. "I want you to fetch water from the river with my basket and fill the big clay pot standing behind the house."

The young man was amazed at such a difficult request. Nevertheless, he did not give up but grabbed the reed basket and headed down the forest path to the river. Several times he dipped the basket in the water, but it all ran out the moment he lifted it. Disappointed and terribly frustrated, he wondered what to do next.

Meanwhile, Usidiu, upon hearing her father's first task for the Sun Prince, knew it would be impossible. Since, like her father, she possessed some magical powers, she knew she must help him. So she quietly slipped away from her room and ran down to the riverside to offer her assistance.

Spotting Usidiu, Yar asked, "What can I do, Usidiu? It seems I may never have you for my wife."

"Just let me touch the basket," she said.

Immediately it changed into a basket made of skin—without any holes! Yar finally managed to fetch water to fill the huge clay pot.

When the task was completed, Usidiu, who hid near the big pot, touched the basket and changed it back to its original form.

Yar returned to Nahakaboni and handed him the basket. "The pot is filled," he announced.

The old man carefully examined the filled pot and looked at the young man with a puzzled expression. "Someone must have helped you, but your next task will be more difficult. Bring my fishing arrow, which is in my canoe by the river."

Yar thought that task seemed quite easy, so he rushed to Nahakaboni's canoe, which was tied to a stump.

Surprisingly, he saw no fishing arrow but instead spotted an alligator lying across the canoe, while a large snake lay curled up at the bottom.

Since Yar was considerably afraid of alligators and snakes, he kept his distance from the canoe. Shortly thereafter, Usidiu appeared in the bushes beside him.

"What will I do this time?" he asked. "It seems I can't carry out the second task."

With a broad smile, she tossed a pebble into the canoe. Instantly, the alligator was transformed into a canoe seat, while the snake miraculously changed into a fishing arrow. Yar hurriedly picked up the arrow and took it to Nahakaboni.

"Someone must have helped you," Nahakaboni declared again. "Nevertheless, for your final task, you must shoot the big *lukanani* in the river, but you must shoot the arrow into the air and with your back to the river."

Yar felt the last task was surely hopeless. Everyone knew the big magical lukanani could only be killed by someone who was skilful enough to shoot it with his back to the river. Although many hunters and fishermen tried to kill it in the past, they all had failed miserably.

Despite this, Yar gathered his bow and arrows and walked to the riverbank. At the same time, he pondered how to go about performing such difficult tasks since he possessed no hunting skills.

But, as before, Usidiu was waiting for him by the riverbank with an arrow in her hand. "Take this magic arrow and fit it to your bow," she explained. "Turn your back to the river and shoot the arrow above your head. But make sure that your eyes are closed."

He cautiously followed her instructions and, after a few seconds, hesitantly opened his eyes. Amazingly, he saw the lukanani floating on the river surface with his arrow stuck to its side. In no time, he leaped forward and grabbed the fish. He then gave back Usidiu the magic arrow, which she took home.

Shortly after, he fetched the fish to Nahakaboni.

"My dear young man," the old man said, "either someone helped you, or you yourself have great magical powers. As I promised, I will give you my daughter as your wife."

There was great rejoicing among the forest people as they and Nahakaboni celebrated the grand wedding of Yar and the beautiful Usidiu.

A big clay pot

~ 9 ~

Yar's Tasks

Yar and his wife Usidiu lived happily together not far from her father's house, and almost every day, she and her husband would help the old man with some of his chores. It was not unusual in those times for the son-in-law to carry out various tasks for the father-in-law, for such was the tradition of the people of that village.

But Nahakaboni, despite his son-in-law's kindness, always found fault with whatever the young man did for him. He never seemed satisfied.

One day Nahakaboni told Yar, "I want you to help me with a special task."

"What help do you want?" Yar responded. "You know I'm always ready to assist you."

"Just on the edge of the village, I have a field which is full of bushes," the old man said. "I want you to weed it for me."

So the very next day, Yar went to the abandoned field, which was covered with tall, thick bushes. He put his shoulders to the task, and by late afternoon, the entire job was completed. That evening he told his father-in-law, "Your field is now clear, and you can go and inspect it."

"I'll go to see it tomorrow morning," grumbled the old man.

Early the next morning, he departed to inspect the field; but when he returned home, he reported—as usual—that he was far from satisfied.

Yar and Usidiu were not happy with the old man's comments, so they immediately rushed off to see where the work had failed and were shocked to discover all the tall bushes and weeds growing luxuriantly on the plot as before. Little did they know that Nahakoboni, by using his magic powers, had caused the vegetation to grow back again.

Trying his best to please the old man, Yar spent the entire day cutting down the bushes. But the same mystery repeated itself, and his father-in-law once again expressed his displeasure.

"You surely are not doing the task given to you, or else the entire field would have been clear of the bushes," he admonished his son-in-law.

"How did this happen?" Yar, with great frustration, asked his wife. "I cut the field twice, and yet your father is not satisfied. And the bushes grow back as if by magic!"

Usidiu considered the situation for a few moments.

"I'm sure he is using his magic to deter you," she agreed.

"We have to think of a way to overcome his magic powers," Yar suggested.

Usidiu thought about this for a moment.

"My magic powers can't overcome those of my father, so I can't help you with this problem," she explained. But then she finally advised her husband, "Tomorrow, when you go to cut the bushes for a third time, you should uproot the stumps."

So the next day, after Yar had cut down the tall bushes, he took his wife's advice and began the task of uprooting the stumps. But he found that undertaking extremely difficult and failed to uproot even one. In great exhaustion, he fell on his back and cried in disappointment, "I give up. I can't do the job, and Nahakoboni will never be pleased with me."

Just then, a short chubby *hebu*—a forest spirit—appeared by his side.

"What seems to be your problem?" the hebu inquired.

Realizing that this was a friendly hebu, Yar explained the situation to him.

"Don't worry at all, my dear young man," the hebu stated. "I will help you overcome this problem, especially since I never liked that old man."

"What should I do?" Yar asked.

"You don't have to do anything," the hebu explained. "You just have to return home and tell the old man that the field is now fully cleared. Leave everything to me."

Yar followed the friendly hebu's advice and hoped that everything would turn out well.

The following morning, Nahakoboni went to inspect the field; but this time, there was no regrowth as the previous days. With great disappointment, he knew that his magic powers had failed him this time. Late that evening when he returned home, he did not utter a single word to either his daughter or Yar, both of whom were waiting anxiously for him.

Puzzled by Nahakaboni's behavior and anxious to see if the hebu had helped him, Yar and Usidiu visited the field the next morning and were amazed to find—in place of the empty field—large beds of cassava, plantains, and yams growing profusely. It was obvious that the old man had spent the day in planting the crops and had used his magic powers to enable them to grow up quickly.

Nahakoboni knew he had lost this battle of wits with his son-in-law, but he had one final task for him.

"I'm not satisfied with my house," he grumbled. "I want you to build a new one for me."

Yar knew it would be another difficult task, but he had to try again to please the old man; and within a week, Yar erected a new house for him. But the old man was still not satisfied. He dismantled the building and demanded, "Make me a stronger house."

By the riverside later that evening, when the young man was contemplating on the type of house to build, his friend, the chubby hebu, appeared.

"You seem to have more problems, my friend," he observed.

Yar was overjoyed to see him and explained his predicament. The hebu thought for a while and finally said, "You should build a house with the wood of the purpleheart tree. That wood is strong and hard, and the old man will definitely be satisfied with a house made of such material."

Heeding this advice, Yar went into the forest the following day and cut down a large purpleheart tree. With the large amount of wood it provided, he managed to erect a very strong house for Nahakoboni. As soon as it was completed, the old man came across to examine it thoroughly. Now obviously satisfied, he stated, "Yes. This is a strong house which will last a long, long time."

From that day, Nahakoboni ceased making demands of his son-in-law.

A forest farm

~ 10 ~

Makonaima and Pia

Yar and his beautiful wife Usidiu continued to live happily in their small house by the riverside. Then early one morning, Yar informed Usidiu of his upcoming hunting trip into the forest.

"My dear wife," he said, "don't leave the house. You'll soon give birth to our child at any time now."

She faithfully promised him to remain inside while she stood by the door and waved good-bye to him. She watched as he walked through the woods until he disappeared in the darkness of the forest.

While her husband was gone, Usidiu kept herself busy by cleaning the house and mending clothing. But by noon that day, she discovered that he had forgotten to take the meal she had prepared for him. The neatly wrapped parcel of dried meat and farine was still on the kitchen table.

Thinking of how hungry he would be, she picked up the parcel and hurriedly set out along a narrow pathway into the forest with the hope that she would quickly encounter her husband. Soon, she discovered that there were many more similar pathways in the forest, so she began shouting her husband's name while crossing from one pathway to the next, without luck. Exhausted, she decided to return home.

But no matter how much she tried, she could not find her way out of the forest. In despair, she realized she was hopelessly lost. While she made several attempts to find her way home, every new attempt led her deeper and deeper into the dense forest

As night approached, she came upon a little hut among the huge trees. Her spirits lifted, for she felt that she would get help from whoever lived there.

She reached out, tapped the door, and called out, "Please help me. I'm lost in the forest."

The door opened, and an old woman stepped out. "My name is Nanyoba," she croaked. "Come into my hut and rest. You look weak, hungry, and ill."

Usidiu cautiously entered the hut, sat on a low stool, and unfolded her dilemma to Nanyoba.

"My dear girl," said the old woman, "I've lived my entire life in this forest, and I myself don't know the way out. But I'm sure your husband will search for you. He'll find you safe here."

She offered Usidiu a hot meal of boiled sweet potatoes and a cup of casiri to drink. Shortly after Usidiu ate, she felt ill.

That very evening, she gave birth to twin boys. However, she was so ill and weak that she became unconscious. Even though Nanyoba tried to help her, Usidiu died late that night while the moon was high above the trees.

Meanwhile, Nanyoba—who was a wicked witch—always longed for children to work for her. For this reason, she decided to keep the twins and let them believe that she was their mother.

Early the next morning, she buried Usidiu in a deep hole, which she dug behind the hut. After feeding the twins on cassava milk, she named them Makonaima and Pia.

Two days later, while Yar wandered in search of his dear wife, he came to Nanyoba's hut and asked whether she saw her.

"I haven't seen anyone for two months," Nanyoba shamelessly lied.

In the meanwhile, Makonaima and Pia grew up quickly. By the time they were sixteen years old, they were handsome youths, skilled in hunting and fishing. They also discovered that they possessed magical powers, but little did they know that these were inherited from their lovely mother.

And soon, they sensed something mysterious about Nanyoba.

"She never cooks with a fire for us to see," Makonaima told Pia. So they became determined to see how the old woman cooked their meals.

One morning, Nanyoba ordered the boys to gather some firewood. Shortly after they left for the firewood, Makonaima changed himself magically into a lizard, came back, and climbed up the wall to an open window. What he witnessed amazed him.

The old woman was spitting fire and swallowing it again.

He transformed himself back and ran to Pia with his discovery.

"She's a wicked witch!" Pia exclaimed. "We must kill her. She's evil."

"I don't think she's our mother," Makonaima said. "She never wants to talk about our father."

During the night, the boys slipped away from the hut and piled dry branches around it. They started a raging fire, which rapidly engulfed the hut with Nanyoba inside.

Surprisingly, the old witch did not die. Instead, she changed herself into a frog with scorched and wrinkled skin.

It is said that as she burned, the fire she kept in her body jumped out of her mouth and hid in a *hima-hera* tree that grew nearby. Today, if two hima-hera sticks are rubbed together, they quickly produce fire.

Shooting fish

~ 11 ~

Makonaima and Pia Meet Their Father

After burning Nanyoba, Makonaima and Pia decided to search for their father. Since they did not know their real mother, they knew that finding their father would be very difficult.

As they roamed the forest, they inquired about their parents from people and animals they encountered.

Everyone they met gave the same answer: "No, I do not know your parents."

One afternoon, the boys shot two *powis* with their bows and arrows and intended to cook them for dinner.

"These aren't enough," Pia said. "Let's shoot another."

Just then, they saw another powis on a nearby tree. As Makonaima aimed his arrow, the bird spoke. "Please don't shoot me! If you spare my life, I'll tell you about your parents."

Makonaima became excited. "I promise to spare your life and the lives of all powis in the future if you do."

The powis was so grateful that it revealed the whole story about their parents.

"Your father is alive," the bird told them. "He lives on the edge of the forest on the riverbank. He still grieves for your mother, Usidiu, and also for the child or children she was expecting. Even though he can't have her back, he will be happy to have both of you even though he doesn't know you."

"How will he know us?" asked Pia.

"That is easy," replied the bird. "Makonaima, you look just like your father, while you, Pia, are the exact image of your mother."

"Thank you very much, Powis," the boys said. "We will go to meet our father now."

After walking for several days, they arrived at the edge of the forest. There, on the riverbank, was Yar, the Sun Prince. Now a middle-aged man, he sat on a log near his house and gazed as the river gently flowed.

"Father!" they shouted in unison.

Yar turned his head slowly. There was no mistaking the boys. One was the striking image of Usidiu, while the other looked just like him during his boyhood days.

"You are my sons!" he exclaimed, and rushed to embrace them warmly.

"Yes, Father," they replied with excitement.

Afterward, they sat together and revealed their entire stories to each other. The boys told of their life with Nanyoba and their search for their parents. In turn, the father told of his search for Usidiu through the forest and how Nanyoba fooled him. Indeed, he was deeply saddened to hear of his beloved wife's death. "I will always love your mother, and even though she is dead, I have both of you to remind me of her," he told his sons.

At last, Makonaima and Pia remained with their father. Soon, all the people regarded them as the greatest hunters in the land.

The powis

~ 12 ~

The Creation of Mount Roraima

Deep within the forest stood a massive tree. This tree was very unusual because its magical qualities enabled it to produce all kinds of fruits on its wide leafy branches. It also had an immense trunk and was much taller than any other tree, rising like a majestic mountain in the middle of the forest. Large knots protruded from its bark, and its branches were so thickly covered with leaves that they blocked the sunlight from reaching the ground. Nevertheless, it was always full of life since large flocks of birds and swarms of insects occupied its branches and fed on its delicious fruits, which emitted a pleasant fragrance all around. All the people in the surrounding countryside came to this special tree for its abundant supply of fruits, and most of them felt that they must make special efforts to ensure that it was carefully protected. For its colossal size and magical properties, it was known as the Tree of Life.

But Pia, the well-known powerful and muscular woodcutter, was determined to test his skills by cutting down this mammoth tree. One day, he expressed his thoughts to the men in his village.

"All over the land, everyone would regard me as the greatest woodcutter if I chop down this tree," he boasted.

But Akuri, the short rotund farmer, immediately objected to his plan.

"How can you ever think of cutting down the Tree of Life?" he remonstrated. "It provides fruits for us all year round. If you chop it down, we will lose a most valuable resource. And, furthermore, our ancestors warned us that if ever that tree is cut down, a destructive flood will spread all over the land."

But Pia shook his head in disbelief.

"It's just an old superstition that cutting down the tree will bring about a flood," he declared. "I don't believe that will ever happen. And if I cut down the tree, we can easily transplant pieces of its branches all over the land, thus enabling more fruits to be available after a little while."

Opinion was divided over his statement, and while some agreed with him, others—including Akuri—continued to raise objections.

But nothing could deter Pia; so he grabbed his heavy axe, threw it across his broad shoulders, and strode into the forest toward the magic tree. Akuri, worried as ever, hustled behind and pleaded with him to desist from any rash action.

Soon after, Pia arrived at the magic tree and stood beside its huge trunk under the thick branches looming overhead. He lifted his axe and made a heavy chop on the trunk, but the wood was so hard that the heavy axe bounced back without leaving a mark on it. Again and again he swung the axe, but it had no effect at all.

Standing close by, Akuri pleaded for Pia to stop his madness, but the woodcutter ignored him and continued to chop away.

As Pia saw he was making no headway, he suddenly remembered that he could call on the forest spirit to soften the wood of the magic tree. This he did, and almost at once, the forest spirit who had always protected him softened the wood and the heavy axe began to cut deep into the trunk.

Seeing this, Akuri begged, "Please, Pia, don't cut down the tree or else a dangerous flood will emerge from it."

But Pia continued to ignore him, so in frantic haste, he began to collect beeswax and fallen fruits—which he stuffed into the sharp gashes the axe made on the tree trunk. Akuri hoped that his action would prevent any flood that he feared would spew from the damaged tree. But as fast as Akuri kept filling the gashes, Pia continued to hew away at the tree trunk.

Then Pia's axe sank far into the trunk, which had become as soft as a papaya tree, and at any moment it seemed as if the tree would tumble over. By this time, a large crowd of people had gathered at the scene, and they watched as Pia chopped away while Akuri tried desperately to stuff the deep cuts with wax and fruits.

Soon the great tree began to sway, but just as it was about to fall, the onlookers heard a loud shout. It was Anzik, Pia's close friend, who came rushing up to save the Tree of Life. He had been away from the village and, on his return, had learned from some children of what his friend intended to do.

He shouted to the forest spirit, who was his protector as well, to make the tree trunk as hard as rock. At once, the forest spirit heeded his call and, immediately, Pia's axe no longer had any effect on the tree.

But the damage was already done. With the trunk cut more than halfway across, the mighty tree swayed and then crashed heavily to the ground with a loud creaking sound. Its wide-spreading, heavy branches knocked over all trees nearby, and its fruits flew off in all directions. And as it slammed to the ground, the force of its weight split a large section of the trunk and tore up the deeply embedded roots that erupted from the soil, causing a destructive earthquake all over the land. Great blocks of rock were ripped up and thrown in the air as well, and as they fell back, they formed a range of high mountains stretching as far as the eye could see.

As for the enormous trunk of the Tree of Life, it rose up to the sky in the form of a massive rock and created a towering mountain, which later became known as Roraima.

And from its base where the ripped-open trunk once stood, a gigantic spout of water shot out and began to flood the entire countryside. While Pia and some of the villagers saved themselves by rushing to higher ground, many people and animals in the surrounding areas could not escape the deluge. The flow was so fast and furious that large numbers of them drowned because they could not reach high land quickly enough.

One of those lucky enough to escape was Akuri. He ran as fast as he could, but his short chubby legs proved to be a disadvantage. As the floodwaters were almost upon him, the forest spirit mercifully transformed him into an *acouri*, and his newfound swiftness of feet enabled him to scamper rapidly up the steep side of Mount Roraima, high above the raging waters of the mighty flood.

Mount Roraima

The acouri

~ 13 ~

Why There Are Storms on Mount Roraima

Many years ago, the Sun King entered into the business of rearing fish, and soon he created several fishponds on Earth. Occasionally, he visited these ponds to catch some fish. However, while he was away, people or wild animals raided the ponds, so he never caught a satisfactory amount for himself.

After one of his several trips to gather some fish, he discovered what was going on; so he employed Yamuri, the lizard, to keep a close watch on his ponds.

But Yamuri was awfully lazy and loved to sleep in the warm sun. While he slept, people and the forest animals seized the opportunity to continue stealing huge amounts of fish from the ponds.

Learning about this, the Sun King became terribly annoyed with Yamuri. He fired the lizard immediately.

The Sun King then visited the home of Alligator.

"Alligator, I want to employ you as watchman to take care of my fishponds," said the Sun King.

"Why do you think I'd be a good watchman?" asked Alligator.

"Well, you see, you can swim in the ponds. And when thieves come, you'll be there to catch them," explained the Sun King.

Alligator agreed to take the job; and the Sun King left, feeling pleased that, this time, he had found a capable watchman.

Instead, Alligator—who liked the taste of fish so much—became the worst thief that ever robbed the ponds.

When the Sun King came again to Earth to fish, he discovered his ponds had even less fish than before. And there in the middle of a pond was Alligator—with a fish in his mouth!

The Sun King exploded with anger. "You're the worst of thieves!" he yelled at Alligator and slashed him with a *cutlass*. Every part of Alligator's body that received a cut formed a scar that looked like a large scale. Even to this day, all alligators bear those same marks.

After Alligator was hurt, he ran away to the swamps to nurse his wounds. Indeed, he was terrified of the Sun King. So to beg the king's forgiveness, he sent his cousin Iguana with a message.

"Alligator is very sorry for eating your fish," Iguana told the Sun King. "To pay you back, he offers his daughter as your wife."

By then, the Sun King's temper had cooled. In the meanwhile, a few days earlier, his sister, the Moon Princess, had advised him to take a wife to care for him. Alligator's offer, therefore, came at the perfect time.

"Go and tell Alligator I will accept his daughter," he told Iguana. "But that doesn't mean he's allowed near any of my fishponds."

Iguana relayed the news to Alligator, who became very worried. He never expected the Sun King to accept his offer, for he had no daughter to give him! What could he do?

Gradually, Alligator came up with a plan. He carved a wild plum tree into the shape of a woman and begged the Water Spirit to breathe life into it. Feeling sorry for Alligator, the Water Spirit put life into the woman, and Alligator immediately sent his new daughter to the Sun King.

Unfortunately, Alligator's ability to carve was extremely poor, and his daughter looked very ugly indeed. Alligator knew that and feared that the Sun King would be very angry with him for sending such an ugly girl. Because of this, he hid in the swamp, peeking out at the sun to see if the Sun King was looking for him again. Even today, alligators still peek out at the sun from rivers and streams.

The Sun King, who was indeed displeased with Alligator's ugly daughter, kept her as his wife for only a few months. He then left her and never came back. But she loved the Sun King so much that she returned to Earth and searched everywhere for him.

After many weeks of searching, she still could not find her husband. Late one afternoon, she arrived at Mother Toad's house deep in the forest.

"What are you doing here?" Mother Toad asked.

"My husband, the Sun King, left me. I'm searching for him," replied Alligator's daughter.

"You won't find him," said Mother Toad. "When he wants to hide, no one ever finds him."

The girl cried bitterly, and Mother Toad felt sorry for her.

"Why don't you live with me?" Mother Toad suggested.

The girl considered the offer for a while, and then nodded. "My husband doesn't want to live with me. It might be best if I stay away from him and live with you."

At the time when she went to live with Mother Toad, the Sun King's wife was pregnant. Soon after she moved in with Mother Toad, she gave birth to twin boys, whom she named Makonaima and Pia. They were as handsome as their father.

The boys grew up under their mother's care at Mother Toad's home. And through their natural ability, they became very skilled hunters and fishermen.

One day, Mother Toad's son Tiger—who lived in another part of the forest—came to visit. That was the first time he saw the twins and their mother.

But before leaving for home, Tiger proposed marriage to the twins' mother. She refused instantly, and that made Tiger extremely angry. With a frightening roar, he jumped and slapped her with all his might and then ran away. She fell unconscious, and without the proper care she received from her sons and Mother Toad, she would have certainly died. After a few weeks, she recovered and was able to do her work in the home once again.

For all these reasons and more, her sons developed a strong hatred for Tiger. And as they hunted one afternoon, they shot Tiger with their poison arrows. Tiger did not die immediately, but suffered miserably for three days from terrible pains caused by the poisonous arrows. Then he finally succumbed.

One day, Makonaima said to his mother, "Pia and I are old enough now to be on our own. It's time I leave Mother Toad's house and travel throughout the land. I'd like Pia and you to accompany me." Both she and Pia agreed.

They sadly bade farewell to Mother Toad before setting out on an extended journey through the dense forest. On their way, Makonaima decided to cut down a huge *crabwood* tree from the bank of a large river, which he shaped into a canoe. This they used to travel across the numerous rivers they encountered.

During the course of their travels, Makonaima and Pia developed a new way to catch fish. They removed large boulders from the riverbanks and placed them in the river's swiftly flowing waters. The boulders, in turn, blocked the flowing waters, thus preventing the fish from moving downstream. As the fish got trapped near the rocks, the boys were able to shoot many of them effortlessly. These they cooked for their meals.

However, after making their catch, the boys were forgetful and left the rocks in the river. Over time, these formed huge rapids and waterfalls.

In the meantime, Crane—the tall long-legged bird—followed Makonaima and Pia closely for all the fish the brothers discarded. Soon he and the brothers developed a close friendship, but this friendship eventually led to a serious quarrel between the two brothers.

Pia continually accused Crane of eating too many of the fish they caught. But Makonaima defended Crane, saying that was not true. Eventually, the quarrel became so unbearably bitter between the two brothers that they decided to go their separate ways. As expected, Makonaima took Crane with him.

Meanwhile, Pia and his mother remained together. He faithfully took care of her and supplied her with meat, fish, and fruit. As she grew older, he built a little hut for them at the summit of Mount Roraima. Occasionally, Pia left home and went to the lowland villages to teach the people different skills. And as time went by, all the learned men who taught others these same skills became known as *piamen*.

Finally, Pia left the villages and returned to his mother on Mount Roraima.

"Mother," he told her, "I have finished my work of teaching the people all they must know. Now I shall leave you to go to another place far away to teach others. I won't return this time, but I won't leave you in want. If you ever need something, all you have to do is bow your head, cover your face with your hands, and wish for whatever you want and, through my magic powers, you will receive it."

Then he sadly left his mother after bidding her a fond farewell.

To this day, his mother remains on Mount Roraima. She still makes her wishes, but when she thinks of her two sons and husband who deserted her, she becomes overwhelmed with sadness and cries bitterly. Whenever this happens, her tears sweep through the mountainside in a heavy rainstorm. As they flow steadily, they form streams that run down the steep slopes to join the rivers that flow through the forest to the great Atlantic Ocean.

The Iguana

The Alligator

~ 14 ~

Boona, Mayorokoto, and Tiger

Boona was a beautiful girl who lived alone in a little house in a village near the forest. Her parents died a few years before, and even though some villagers wanted her to live with them, she preferred living alone in her little house. She cultivated her own little farm on the edge of the forest some distance from her home. From the nearby creeks, she often caught fish, but other villagers sometimes gave her meat from animals they killed in the forest.

One afternoon, Boona went to her farm to uproot some cassava. After collecting a basketful, she began clearing away some of the weeds she found growing everywhere. Since it was getting late, she planned to return the next day to complete the task.

Early the next morning, she returned to her farm, prepared for a hard day's work. What she saw absolutely surprised her. All the weeds had vanished, and fresh cassava sticks, to generate new plants, were planted in the places where she uprooted cassava the previous day.

"There is a very kind person here," she said to herself. "I'll be very glad to meet and thank that person."

From that day onward, Boona's farm remained as neat as ever.

Weeds were removed the moment they sprouted, plants were watered, and when it was reaping time, the cassava or sweet potatoes were neatly heaped up in a corner of the farm.

Boona wondered who did all that hard work. Even though she spent several whole days at her farm, she was never lucky to see her helper.

After giving some thoughts to these mysterious happenings, Boona concluded that her helper came at night to work. She therefore decided to stay overnight at the farm to see who it was. So she spent an entire day at the farm, and as darkness began to slowly creep in, she hid in a clump of bushes on the edge of the farm and waited patiently.

At around midnight, she heard leaves rustling and light footsteps. From her hiding place, she cautiously peeked out. Out of the bushes stepped a handsome young man. Boona became breathless as she watched him walk to where some sweet potatoes had recently been harvested. Very quietly and skillfully, he shaped the sweet potato beds on which he planted sweet potato *slips*.

Boona, anxious to meet him, got out of her hiding place and walked up to the young man. Upon hearing her approaching footsteps, he immediately spun around to face her.

"So you are the mysterious person who's been doing all the work on my farm," Boona said.

"Yes, Boona. I never wanted you to know," the young man replied.

"Why? But I must thank you very much. You have helped me a great deal. How can I thank you for all you've done?" asked Boona.

"I don't need any thanks. I've been doing all this because I have secretly loved you for a long time. My name is Mayorokoto, and I live in another part of the forest. We've never met. If you really wish to thank me, you can agree to be my wife," replied the young man.

Boona readily agreed to the proposal, and a few days later, they got married. They lived together in her little house, and during the day, they worked on their farm. Not long after, they got a son and named him Haburi.

Boona and her family lived happily together, but soon this happiness was shattered. It happened when Mayorokoto left home early one morning to fish.

After trying for many tedious hours, he could not catch any fish.

"Today must be a bad day for fishing here," he said. "I know what I'll do—I'll fish in Tiger's creek."

True, there was a creek nearby that actually belonged to Tiger, and it was full of fish, but people were afraid to fish there. Boona had often warned Mayorokoto not to fish in Tiger's creek, but that morning he did not heed her warning. He went to Tiger's creek, and he was busy placing *haiarri* roots in the water to stun the fish when Tiger leaped from the bushes. He dealt two heavy slaps on Mayorokoto that killed him instantly.

Tiger then dragged the dead body to the bank. Shortly thereafter, he collected all the stunned fish floating in the water and packed them in Mayorokoto's *quake*.

Then suddenly, Tiger looked at Mayorokoto's body and began to laugh hysterically. "So you are the husband of the beautiful Boona. I've always wanted her for my wife. Since you are dead, I'll now take your place."

Since Tiger possessed magical powers, he was able to quickly change himself into a man who looked exactly like Mayorokoto. Then he picked up the quake full of fish and proceeded to Boona's house.

Meanwhile, Boona was busy in her kitchen baking cassava bread when the disguised Tiger entered the house. The baby, Haburi, was crying while creeping on the floor.

"Mayorokoto," Boona called, "I know you're tired, but please look after Haburi until I'm finished in the kitchen."

Without delay, Tiger obediently picked up the crying baby and sat in Mayorokoto's hammock. Soon, he fell asleep and began snoring very loudly.

Hearing the snores, Boona was shocked, for her husband never snored that loudly before. In the meantime, Tiger was dreaming of how he killed Mayorokoto. All of a sudden, he shouted in his sleep, "Mayorokoto, I killed you. Boona is my wife now!"

Upon hearing this, Boona became awfully frightened. She was certain that was not her husband in the hammock. She instantly recognized Tiger's voice as he spoke. He must have killed Mayorokoto and used magic to change his shape, she reasoned.

She had to escape with Haburi immediately. So, moving quietly to the hammock, she cautiously released Haburi from Tiger's arms and, instead, substituted in them a bundle of cotton. And without a moment's delay, she slipped from the house with Haburi and ran toward the house of Wowta, the old witch, who was her closest neighbor. But Wowta's house was quite some distance away.

Shortly after Boona left, Tiger woke up. He saw that instead of the baby, he was holding on to a bundle of cotton. He soon became conscious, too, that Boona knew who he was; so he changed himself back to his original shape and rushed out of the house just in time to see Boona running toward Wowta's house with the baby. He roared loudly and raced after them.

As Boona reached Wowta's house, she screamed, "Wowta, open the door and let me in! I'm trying to escape from Tiger."

From inside, the old witch shouted back, "No, I don't want anyone coming in my house."

Boona trembled fearfully as she heard Tiger's roar close behind her. She turned and saw him rushing toward her. Suddenly, she got an idea. She pinched Haburi, who began to cry very loudly. This caused Wowta to open the door in a flash.

"Come in," she said. "I don't like hearing babies cry."

Boona dashed inside with the baby and slammed the door quickly.

"Thank you, Wowta. Please save me from Tiger," she begged.

At the same time, Tiger arrived at the door.

"Wowta," he shouted, "I came for Boona and her baby. Put them outside immediately."

But Wowta never liked Tiger. In addition to being a bully, he performed magic, and she was jealous of anyone else who did so.

"Boona and her baby are not here!" she shouted.

"I saw them enter the house just a moment ago," Tiger screamed.

Just then Wowta opened the door slightly and said to Tiger, "If you don't believe me, push your head through the door and see for yourself."

The edge of the door was lined with long sharp thorns. As soon as Tiger pushed his head through the small space, Wowta promptly slammed the door. The sharp thorns stabbed Tiger and, in no time, he fell down dead.

Later, Wowta and Boona buried Tiger. When they were finished, Wowta said, "Look here, Boona, I killed Tiger for you. In repayment, you must live with me. I'm getting old, and I need help with the housework."

Boona was forced to agree, and from then onward, she and Haburi lived with Wowta. While the old witch prepared magical charms for people, Boona cooked meals, collected firewood, and cultivated a small garden near the house. She took care of her baby and hoped that someday he would grow up to be a strong, handsome man like his father.

Cassava bread drying on the rooftop

~ 15 ~

The Struggles of Haburi

One morning, Boona went to her farm to collect cassava while Wowta took care of Haburi. However, the old witch had other plans. Using her magical powers, she transformed Haburi into a young man.

"You will be my slave," she told him.

When Boona returned home in the afternoon, she searched the house but could not find her baby anywhere. All she saw were Wowta and a young man. Little did she know that the young man was her own dear son.

"Where's Haburi?" Boona distrustfully questioned Wowta.

"Maybe he crept outside while I was resting," the old witch answered casually. "Someone must have carried him away. Never mind the baby. Here's a young man I found. He'll be my slave."

Boona looked curiously at the young man. He stared back at her. However, because of the magical change he endured, he could not recognize his mother.

Boona continued her search for her baby everywhere, but she could not find him. Even though she cried bitterly and was deeply hurt, she refrained from picking a quarrel with Wowta for her carelessness because she feared the witch would harm her.

From then on, Wowta sent Haburi on daily hunting trips. He always returned with much game, but the old witch made sure that Boona got the smallest birds or animals, while Wowta always kept the best for herself.

During the course of his hunting trips, Haburi took time off to swim in the rivers. Soon, he made friends with the *water-dogs* that lived there. Since then, he always looked forward to his daily swim with them.

As he rested on the riverbank after a long swim one afternoon, an old water-dog came up beside him and said, "Young man, there's something important that you should know."

"What is it?" inquired Haburi.

The old water-dog explained: "First, you must know that the old woman, Wowta, who sends you to hunt every day, is a witch. Secondly, Boona—the woman who lives with you—is really your mother. You were only a baby a few weeks ago, but Wowta's magic changed you into a young man so you'd be her slave. Your mother doesn't know that you are Haburi, her son. She believes that her baby was lost through Wowta's carelessness."

Haburi was thankful to the water-dog for the information.

That evening, when he returned home, he witnessed Wowta giving Boona the smallest fish he brought. They all ate dinner, and shortly after, Wowta went to the edge of the forest in search of herbs for her magic spells.

While the witch was gone, Boona washed the dishes.

"Did you have an interesting day today?" she asked Haburi.

"Yes, I did," replied Haburi. "I met an old water-dog who told me I am Haburi, and you're my mother. He told me that Wowta changed me from a baby to a young man so I'd be her slave."

Boona was shocked. Eventually, she grabbed Haburi's hand and said softly, "I believe what you said. Water-dogs never lie, and they always know people's secrets."

Boona explained to her son how they came to be living with Wowta.

"Even though she saved us from Tiger," Haburi said, "she made sure she'd use us as her slaves. She's wicked. I must kill her. If I don't kill her, we'll be her slaves the rest of our lives."

Later, when Wowta returned home, Haburi and Boona pretended to be strangers.

The next morning, Wowta told Haburi, "Today you'll cut wood in the forest, and I will go with you to collect herbs."

Haburi contemplated the idea, for he knew that was a good chance to kill the witch. Soon they set out on their journey, and while she searched for the herbs under the trees, he cut a kookrit palm and made it fall on her. Though the blow was heavy, it did no harm to the witch, for she was protected by her magical powers.

Still, she was angry and suspicious of Haburi.

"You made that tree fall on me, didn't you?" she screamed angrily.

"Yes, I did," he snapped. "I hate you for what you did to me and my mother."

"So you know my secret, do you?" laughed the witch wickedly. "Well, you'll continue to be my slave, and I'll make sure you never escape. My magic will ensure that you stay with me and return even when I send you hunting."

Haburi was fully aware that he could not kill the witch by ordinary means. He therefore must make some other attempt to escape. This opportunity came one day when Wowta sent him on a long journey to the Atlantic Ocean to collect crabs on the beach. Upon arrival at the seashore, he collected large pieces of driftwood and hurriedly constructed a raft. He then climbed onto the raft and pushed away from land using a long pole.

"I'm free!" he shouted excitedly.

As the raft glided smoothly across the water, a thought crossed Haburi's mind. He must, without delay, find a more powerful magician than Wowta to free his mother from the evil witch.

Just at that moment, huge waves forcefully pushed his raft back to shore. He soon realized what was happening. His attempt to escape had failed miserably.

"I'm sure Wowta's magic made those waves drive me back," he said.

Disappointedly, he collected a quake of crabs and went home.

"How did you enjoy the waves?" Wowta jeered. "I told you that you can't escape from me!"

But Haburi was determined more than ever to free himself and his mother from the old witch. Not long after, he came up with another escape plan. This time, he carefully collected wax from wild beehives in the forest and secretly shaped a wax canoe on the riverbank. After its completion, he gladly pushed the canoe into the river. With a mighty explosion, it suddenly burst into flames. And very quickly, the molten wax was gulped down by the river water.

"That has to be Wowta's work again," he sighed in disgust.

Nevertheless, Haburi did not give up. Many times he constructed wood canoes, but just like before, they always disappeared when he was about to flee. For months, life went on like that for Haburi.

Meanwhile, Wowta—who loved honey—sent Haburi to collect it from the wild beehives in the forest. Every time he did so, he hid the wax he drained.

"I don't believe you're bringing home all the honey you collect," the witch accused him one morning. "I'm going today to see that you get all of it."

Later that day, both Haburi and Wowta set out in search of honey. Soon, Haburi found a hive in a hollow tree trunk near the place where he stored his wax collection. The smell of honey in the tree trunk was so appetizing that Wowta could not wait for Haburi to collect the sweet liquid. She pushed him aside and crept into the hole to enjoy the honey.

At that moment an idea flashed across Haburi's mind. That was his chance to get rid of the witch. While she was in the hole enjoying the honey, he hurriedly gathered his hidden wax and tightly blocked the hole, trapping Wowta inside. She tried desperately to escape, but the hole was tightly sealed. Even her magic powers failed, this time, to set her free.

Meanwhile, in the hive, the angry bees stung her so badly that all she could do to save herself was to change into a frog. As a frog, she immediately lost all her magic powers and remained helplessly imprisoned in the tree.

Haburi quickly made a raft, and he and Boona sailed down the river and escaped from the area where Wowta lived. Eventually, they sailed into the wide Atlantic Ocean and arrived in another land where they lived happily together without fear of the wicked witch.

As for Wowta, she remained as a frog in the hollow tree trunk. Then one day, she finally escaped when the bees dug a hole in the wax blocking the entrance to the hive. As a frog, she wandered in the swamps in search of her slave, Haburi.

To this day, the bumps from the bee stings evidently remain on her skin. She still hops about shouting Haburi's name, but every time she shouts, her voice comes out as an ugly croak.

The otter (Guyana's *water-dog*)

~ 16 ~

The Haiarri Root

Many years ago, there were many Amerindian villages on both banks of the Mazaruni River. As such, the boys and girls who lived there learned to swim at an early age. In fact, everyone in the village knew how to swim except the babies and a few toddlers.

In one of the villages lived a man with his three-year-old son, Haiarri.

Haiarri begged his father one morning to teach him how to swim. The father was ever so happy that his son was taking an interest in swimming that, without delay, he took the boy's hand and, together, they walked to the river for swimming lessons.

As usual, the river was always full of fish. Some were either shot with arrows or trapped by the fishermen of the villages. However, as soon as Haiarri's father arrived and he put the boy in the water, a very strange thing happened! Some of the fish that swam in the vicinity of the boy's body mysteriously became unconscious and floated to the surface!

At first, Haiarri and his father were puzzled to see the fish floating so near to them. But in the end, they gathered and took them home. There they discovered that the fish were fresh, and after Haiarri's mother cleaned them, she prepared a large meal for dinner.

Haiarri's father was excited because he was now aware that the fish became unconscious only when he placed his son in the water.

"This is a good way to catch fish," he told his wife after dinner. "All I have to do is to put Haiarri in the river, and all the fish nearby will float to the surface where can gather them easily."

Ever since that day, Haiarri's father took him to the river where he quickly learned to swim. At the same time, his father collected large amounts of fish without any hard labor.

Because of the boy's strange gift, the fish soon feared that all of them would soon be caught. They therefore summoned an urgent meeting to decide on the new threat to their lives. Many ideas came up. Then they finally decided to attack Haiarri, all at the same time, when he sat on the riverbank. This was the only way they could safely approach him. If he entered the water, no fish could get near him without falling unconscious.

After the meeting, they all kept a close watch on Haiarri's movements. Then one afternoon, they saw him sitting on a log near the water. In a flash, all the fish jumped out of the water simultaneously and stabbed him with their fins, then plunged back into the river. The stingray's stab was the worst—it was poisonous.

"Help me, Father!" Haiarri screamed. "The stingray stabbed me!"

Rushing to help Haiarri, his father saw that his little son was dying. He lifted him up in his arms, and as he rushed home, drops of the boy's blood fell on the ground.

Then another strange thing happened. In every spot where a drop of Haiarri's blood fell, a plant sprang up. That became known as the haiarri plant. Ever since, the people began to use that plant to catch fish. They would cut a piece of the root and place it in a stream. Any fish that went close to that root became unconscious and floated to the surface.

Amerindian mother and children

~ 17 ~

The Braggart

There once was a young man named Bhamoo. Ever since he was a boy, he loved to boast about himself, and he always liked to tell others that he was the best hunter in the land. He also bragged that there was no one stronger than he was.

One bright, sunny day, Bhamoo went to visit relatives who lived in another village. There, they introduced him to the other young men who lived in the neighborhood. These young men were friendly, and so, to entertain Bhamoo, they took him on a frog hunt.

Frog legs were normally used for making a tasty meal in that village, and it was common for the young men to hunt for large frogs that lived among the tall grass on the riverbanks. Each hunter took a hefty piece of wood to hit the frogs.

One young man handed Bhamoo a stick and told him that he had to hit the frogs hard because they were very large. Bhamoo arrogantly tossed the stick away and boasted, "I don't need a weapon to kill a frog. All I have to do is jump on one and wring his neck."

As he boasted to the young men, the king of the frogs heard him and decided to teach him an unforgettable lesson. While in those days, frogs understood the language of people, they could not speak it themselves.

The king of the frogs came up with a plan. He summoned all the frogs that lived near his home and instructed them to croak as loudly as they could, while he himself would pretend to be asleep on the riverbank.

Together the frogs began to croak loudly, and Bhamoo—who, despite his boasting, was really a coward—became afraid. The other young men laughed mockingly at him.

"Don't be afraid, Bhamoo," they told him. "It's only the croaking of the frogs."

"I'm not afraid," replied Bhamoo quickly. "I just never heard so many frogs croak at once before."

Just then, he spotted the huge king of the frogs napping peacefully on the riverbank. Wanting to impress his companions, Bhamoo jumped on the frog's back and threw his arms around its neck.

Instantly, the frog spun around and wrapped his long legs tightly around Bhamoo's body and plunged into the river with him. The frog deliberately kept him under the water for a long while until Bhamoo felt his lungs would burst. The frog then brought the young man back to the surface again.

When Bhamoo's companions saw him disappear into the river for that long, they thought he was drowned. But when the frog brought him up to the surface again, with the frog's legs tightly wrapped around the braggart, they laughed hysterically.

Bhamoo shouted, "Don't stand there and laugh! Come and haul this frog away from me."

"Wring its neck, Bhamoo!" they mocked.

They all stood there and watched as the king of the frogs swam away with Bhamoo and dumped him on the opposite bank. The braggart was highly embarrassed by the way the frog treated him. Because of this, he never returned to his relatives' village again. In fact, he never returned to his own village either. He was afraid people would laugh at him because the frog got the better of him and carried him away.

So he went far away until he found a distant village. There he married and lived to a very old age. He never boasted about anything again and became a respectable member of his community. Whenever he heard a young man boasting, he would call him aside and caution, "Never boast about anything. Be modest, and people will respect you."

A river scene near an Amerindian village

~ 18 ~

The Hunter and the Magician's Daughter

Kassikaitu was a young man who was well-known throughout the land for his hunting skills. Every other day, he went deep into the forest to hunt wild animals and always returned home with a dead animal slung over his broad shoulders. On these trips, he took his hunting dogs, for they were trained to chase and catch the animals he pursued.

Meanwhile, an old magician lived along the same pathway that Kassikaitu took whenever he journeyed into the forest. The magician had a beautiful daughter named Rewa. Every other day, Rewa looked forward to seeing Kassikaitu as he passed by her home and, not long after, fell madly in love with the young hunter.

She dearly hoped to be his wife someday.

Every time the young man returned from his hunt, Rewa stood by the pathway outside her home so that he could see her. Unfortunately, the young hunter never seemed to notice her. He was more concerned with the dead animal on his shoulders or his hunting dogs running beside him.

Eventually, the disappointed young woman told her father of her secret love for Kassikaitu.

"My dear father, I love him very much, but he never looks at me when I stand beside the path," she complained. "He's more concerned with his dogs than with anything else. Maybe I'm not beautiful as others think."

"That's not true, Rewa," her father responded. "You are the most beautiful maiden among our people, and I'm sure he'll notice you someday and will want to marry you."

But regardless how often she stood by the pathway for Kassikaitu to notice her, she always went back inside her home deeply disappointed. He never showed any interest in her.

"Since Kassikaitu only seems to notice his dogs, I want you to use your magic powers and transform me into a hunting dog," she begged her father one evening.

Her father readily agreed, for he was aware how very much Rewa loved the hunter.

He handed her a piece of animal skin and explained, "This is a magic skin. All you do is put it on your shoulders, and instantly, everyone will see you as a hunting dog."

The following morning, as Kassikaitu passed by, Rewa put the magic skin around her shoulders and joined him on his hunting trip through the forest. To everyone, she was just another dog.

What she did was to leave before the end of the hunt, and as the dogs chased a young deer, she grabbed that opportunity to hurriedly slip away to Kassikaitu's home. There, she swept the house clean and baked cassava bread for him before returning to her home.

When Kassikaitu returned home that evening, he was surprised to find his house tidy and a meal of cassava bread waiting for him. He wrongfully assumed that one of his kind neighbors came in to help while he was away from home.

"Who is this kind person?" he wondered.

Every other day, the magically disguised girl joined the young man in only part of the hunt, then she hurried away to do his housework before he arrived home.

He, in turn, continued to believe that one of his neighbors helped him while he was away.

Meanwhile, at her home, Rewa felt a great deal better.

"At least things are a bit better now," she told her father. "I'm near my lover part of the day, even though he doesn't know. Also, I'm glad I can prepare meals for him while he's away."

Not long after, as Kassikaitu and his dogs killed a deer, he somehow noticed that one of his dogs was missing. Of course, it was Rewa, who had slipped off as soon as the other dogs began chasing the deer.

"I wonder what happened to that other dog," he thought. "Maybe it was injured while we chased the deer."

He called the other dogs together, threw the dead deer on his shoulders, and began a thorough search for the missing hunting dog. He never found it, and in the search, he eventually ended up near his home.

"Since we're almost home, we should abandon hunting for the day," he told the dogs.

As he advanced toward his front door, he heard strange sounds inside. He quietly set down the deer and cautiously peeked through the window. He was astounded to see the most beautiful young woman baking cassava bread on the fire.

Indeed, he immediately fell in love with her. Undoubtedly, she must be the one who was secretly doing his chores.

He rushed inside and asked, "Who are you?"

"I am Rewa, the magician's daughter," she replied softly.

"So you are the person who comes to do my housework?" he inquired. "Why?"

Hesitantly, Rewa replied, "I do this because I love you. I have loved you for a long time, but you never noticed me."

"Well, I notice you now, and I truly love you too," Kassikaitu told her. "I'm so glad that I found you while searching for the lost dog, or else I'd still be wondering who was the kind person doing all my chores."

Rewa smiled pleasingly, "You haven't lost a hunting dog. I was the dog in disguise."

She explained the power of the magic skin and how she accompanied him on his hunting trips. She even put on the skin to show him how it worked.

"From today," Kassikaitu told her, "you don't have to come here secretly. Let's go to your father, and I'll ask for permission to marry you."

With that, they set off for Rewa's house, and her father happily welcomed his future son-in-law. They immediately began making wedding preparations, and one week later, Rewa and Kassikaitu were married. They lived happily ever after.

An Amerindian family's house

~ 19 ~

The Old Man's Waterfall

Once upon a time, there was a little village on the Potaro River, just above the huge waterfall now known as Kaieteur. In that same region was a large stretch of grassland where several animals such as deer, bush-hogs, and anteaters lived. Near the village, too, the people cultivated farms of cassava, sweet potatoes, corn, and green vegetables.

During that period, an old man named Kaie lived in the village. As a young man, Kaie was a hard worker, a clever hunter, and a skilled fisherman. Even though farming was not his favorite occupation, he was still able to produce good crops of cassava and corn.

Meanwhile, as Kaie grew considerably old, and like so many old men who worked hard in their youth, he became senile and talked to himself as he walked idly around the village.

No one was eager to chat with him any longer because, by that time, they failed to understand the words he uttered. In addition, he had some huge, unpleasant sores on his feet that seemed to be there forever. To make matters even worse, Kaie became a nuisance. Any time of the day or night, he would enter the home of a villager without invitation and would not leave unless he was asked. Because of this, people constantly complained to each other about his unbearable behavior.

"Old Kaie's disgusting," one man said. "Yesterday, some people from another village came to visit my family. Of all days, Old Kaie chose that day to walk into my home! He sat on the floor, muttering to himself, and with those sores on his feet, you can understand how embarrassed I felt."

"I know how you feel," another man replied. "All of us are suffering from the man's disgusting behavior."

As time passed, old Kaie became a greater nuisance than before.

"Why do we have to work to provide food for him?" a young man asked. "Have you ever seen him when he eats with us? He devours more than three of us!"

After they could stand his behavior no longer, the villagers summoned an urgent meeting to discuss Kaie's attitude. At the meeting, everyone concluded the old man was the worst problem the village ever experienced.

"How can we stop him from being such a nuisance?" a young man asked.

A general discussion ensued over the methods to be used. Some villagers suggested that they should send Kaie away by force, but others strongly disagreed.

"If we do that," they said, "he'll go to another village and pester the people there."

After several other discussions, they finally decided to set Kaie adrift in a canoe on the Potaro River.

"He'll go over the waterfall," they reasoned. "That will be the end of the problem."

Early the next morning when all plans were in place, the villagers placed Kaie in a canoe with his *pegall*—a type of basket—containing everything he owned. Two young men then pushed the little canoe alongside the speeding current of the river as the other villagers stood by the riverbank and watched. The canoe quickly picked up speed, and the raging current pulled it toward the waterfall.

By this time, Kaie became aware of his fate.

"Save me! Save me!" he screamed frightfully. "I promise to be good!"

By then, it was too late. The canoe sped along the river, and the villagers stood and watched in silence from the bank. Nearer and nearer, the canoe drifted toward the waterfall. Old Kaie's screams filled the air, but they were soon drowned out by the roaring water. Then, gracefully, the canoe tumbled over the mighty waterfall and disappeared.

Undoubtedly, Kaie must have died; but surprisingly, his body was never found, even though the men searched thoroughly by the foot of the waterfall to be certain that he died. But a short distance downstream, they discovered a narrow rocky island shaped like an upturned canoe. And curiously, on the riverbank at the foot of the waterfall was a rock shaped like Kaie's pegall.

"Maybe we did something wrong," one of the searchers said. "His canoe and pegall turned into rocks to remind us every day of the wrong we committed."

Ever since, in repentance, the people of the village named the waterfall Kaieteur—the waterfall of Kaie—in honor of the old man.

Even today, the rock formations of an upturned canoe and a pegall can still be seen near the foot of the Kaieteur Falls.

Kaieteur Falls

~ 20 ~

The Girl Who Was Once a Monkey

A long time ago, in the forest on the bank of the Essequibo River, an old hunter caught a young monkey and took it home as his pet. He and his wife took good care of it, and soon, the monkey became closely attached to the couple.

The monkey was born in a family that possessed magical powers, but the old hunter and his wife knew nothing of this.

As time passed, the monkey understandably grew to love the kind couple. Then one day, while the couple went into the forest to hunt birds, the monkey shed its skin and magically transformed itself into a beautiful maiden. As a young lady, she was able to quickly complete all the household chores for the couple.

After preparing a sumptuous meal for the old couple, she changed into a monkey once again.

When the hunter and his wife returned from the forest, they were pleasantly surprised to find all their household chores completed and a delicious meal prepared for them.

"I wonder who was so kind as to do all this," the old woman pondered.

"Maybe someone saw how old we are and came to help us while we were away," the old man suggested.

The next day, the old couple went into the forest to collect firewood this time. When they returned home, they again found all their chores done.

"It's a pity our pet monkey can't speak," the hunter said. "Then we'd know who came to help us while we were away."

Meanwhile, the situation continued like this for many weeks, and the couple wondered who the mysterious person was.

One evening, when the couple returned from a fishing trip and found all the household chores finished and a meal awaiting them, the man whispered to his wife, "The next day we go into the forest, I'll ask my nephew to secretly watch the house and see who comes to do the housework for us."

As the hunter and his wife left for the forest, the nephew, who was a hunter as well, hid in some bushes nearby to find the mysterious person. From there, his view of the house was quite clear for he could see directly through an open window.

Thinking that no one could see her, the monkey hurriedly removed her skin and again changed into a beautiful girl. She grabbed a broom and swept the floor clean.

From his hiding place, the young man was awestruck as he witnessed the weird transformation. As he recovered, he became even more astounded at the girl's unmatchable beauty. He soon knew he was falling in love with her. Not knowing how to tell her, he rushed into the house and grabbed her arm.

"Please don't change back into a monkey," he pleaded. "You are a beautiful girl. I want to marry you."

"If you promise to be kind to me, I'll marry you," she said with a smile.

"How could I ever be unkind?" he asked. "Of course, I promise to be always kind to you."

With that, the girl readily agreed to be his wife. The young man then picked up the monkey skin from the floor and threw it into the kitchen fire where it quickly burned to ashes.

When the old couple returned from the forest later that day, they met their nephew with a beautiful maiden. From their nephew, they learned what had transpired and of the young couple's marriage plans.

"I can't become a monkey again," the girl explained. "My magical monkey skin was destroyed by the fire."

A few days later, they were married, and after a while, they had a beautiful son.

Like before, the girl was very hardworking. She was also considerably kind to her husband. On the other hand, the husband, at first, was kind to his wife; but after the birth of their son, he soon forgot his promise. He expressed displeasure with the food she prepared and, from time to time, insulted her. With this sudden change in her husband's behavior, she became awfully sad. Nevertheless, she remained kind to her husband even though he treated her poorly.

One morning, as she held her baby son in her arms, she told her husband, "I'm taking our son to the river to bathe him."

While her husband grunted a reply, she picked up a *calabash* and went down to the river.

After a few hours passed, she did not return, so her husband became worried and he left the house in search of her. When he arrived at the riverbank, he saw, much to his surprise, his wife walking like a monkey. At the same time, the child was imitating his mother.

"What are you doing?" he screamed angrily as he ran up to her.

"I don't want to live with you anymore," she yelled back at him. "You treat me badly, and I want to be a monkey again."

It was only then that he realized he had become an unkind husband.

"My wife, please forgive me," he begged her. "I'll be kind to you. Please don't leave me."

"You broke your promise once. You'll do it again," she replied.

He tried desperately to grab her, but she quickly leaped onto a tree on the riverbank's edge. Her baby did the same. As they both jumped from tree to tree, her husband followed on the ground beneath, begging her to come back.

Eventually, the mother and her son reached a narrow part of the river. On the other bank, she saw hundreds of lively monkeys on the trees.

"My people!" she shouted, "I want to escape my bad husband and come back with my son."

Without delay, the monkeys on the opposite bank tried to help her. They quickly climbed a very tall tree, and with their combined weight, the tree bent until the girl could reach it from the other side of the river. With her son tightly clutched in her arms, she jumped and grasped the branches. Once again, she was reunited with her monkey relatives while her husband was left on the opposite bank of the river. He never saw his wife and son again.

And on the mighty Essequibo River, there is a particular place where the riverbanks are relatively close to each other. After all these years, that place is still known as Monkey Jump.

A spider monkey

~ 21 ~

The War of the Birds

Long, long ago, men regarded animals as equal to human beings. At that time too, all birds, beasts, and humans understood each other's language; so communication was rather easy. As such, everyone lived peacefully and assisted each other.

During that same period too, Kamoa, a young man from the Rupununi savannah, met a young woman living alone in a house near the foothills of Mount Ayanganna. She was the daughter of King Vulture who lived in Skyland on top of Mount Ayanganna, and because of magical powers she possessed, she could take the form of a human being, or a vulture, as the situation demanded. After Kamoa fell in love with her, she revealed her secret to him, but he did not mind this at all and insisted that he wanted to marry her.

Soon after, they got married and—as it was customary in those days for a young married man to live with his wife's parents—Kamoa moved with his wife to the home of his parents-in-law. There he was warmly welcomed by his wife's relatives who were all huge vultures but who could change themselves into human form whenever they wished.

But after staying with the vultures for a while, Kamoa understandably became very homesick and longed to see his own relatives who lived on the savannah south of the mountain.

One day, he said to his wife, "I want to visit my old home and see my relatives and friends."

"I must tell my father of your request," she replied.

And later that same day, she conveyed her husband's request to her father, King Vulture.

"No!" her father dictated. "He can't go! Our customs clearly say that when someone is married to a member of the vulture family, he must never return to his parents' home."

But despite all this, Kamoa insisted he must visit his parents. In the end, his wife and the other vultures became very angry with him for being so stubborn. As a punishment, they put him to sit on top of a tall *awarra* palm. The trunk of the tree was thickly covered with sharp thorns, which prevented him from climbing down. Because of this, he remained alone in the tree for many weeks.

One day, as a group of spiders arrived to eat the ripe yellow awarra on the tree, they were shocked to find Kamoa sitting among the branches.

"What are you doing here?" they asked.

He quickly explained his quarrel with the vultures and how he became trapped in the tree. Hearing his plight, the spiders at once felt sorry for him. In no time whatsoever, they spun a cord that stretched from the branches of the awarra tree to the foot of the mountain. With the help of this cord, Kamoa managed to climb down effortlessly and return to his parents' home.

Despite the bad treatment he received from the vultures, Kamoa still loved his wife very dearly. He sent many messages with other birds, urging her to live with him in his home on the savannah. But even though she acknowledged that she missed him and loved him still, she could not dare to leave her parents' home and go to him.

"Tell my husband I can't come, because my relatives prevent me," she told the harpy eagle who brought a message from Kamoa.

Kamoa's heart broke when he received this answer, and he cried bitterly. Meanwhile, all the birds on the savannah pitied him, and they became very annoyed with the vultures for their behavior. They eventually came up with a plan.

The harpy eagle explained this to the young man: "All the birds have decided to take you to Skyland. We'll fight the vultures and return your wife to you."

Kamoa dearly wanted to have his wife again, so he agreed to this idea. Early the next morning, all the birds flew up to Skyland. Two huge harpy eagles held Kamoa's arms in their beaks as they flew side by side toward the vultures' home.

As soon as they arrived in Skyland, a great war of the birds took place on the summit of Mount Ayanganna. The homes of the vultures were completely burnt to the ground. In the end, the birds successfully defeated the vultures. However, Kamoa's wife did not survive. She was spitefully killed by her own relatives so she could not return with her husband. Kamoa himself was killed by his son who sided with his mother's relatives.

As the war ended, a terrible quarrel broke out among the victorious birds over how the treasure seized from the vultures should be shared. A serious fight took place between the trumpet bird and the heron. As they wrestled, they rolled in the ashes and stained their feathers. Evidently, to this day, the descendants of the trumpet bird still have gray backs. Those of that particular heron are gray all over.

While the other birds watched the fight, the owl, who stayed in the background, found a small box carefully wrapped in leaves. He sneaked off with it behind some trees and opened it. The box was full of darkness. And as he opened it, the darkness quickly surrounded him. Ever since, the owl has been forced to spend his waking hours in the darkness.

The *kiskadee* did not join the other birds when they invaded Skyland for he was a coward. Instead, he bandaged his head, claiming he was ill so he could stay at home. When the birds eventually returned home, the hawks discovered his trickery and forced him to wear the white bandage around his head as a symbol of his cowardice.

Ever since, the kiskadee still has a white band around his head. And in his anger, he always attacks hawks whenever he sees them.

The vulture

Awarra tree with fruit

~ 22 ~

Kororomanna and the Hebus

Among the Amerindians of the Warrau tribe, one of the greatest hunters was a young man named Kororomanna. While hunting in the forest one day, Kororomanna shot and killed a huge black howler monkey with his bow and arrow. After resting for a while, he threw the dead monkey across his shoulder and set out for home.

Because of the heavy weight of the dead monkey, Kororomanna's pace was slowed down, and he found himself still in the forest as night fell upon the land. Nevertheless, he kept on walking; but since he could not see too well in the dense darkness, he became confused and was hopelessly lost.

Dropping the dead monkey to the ground, Kororomanna quickly erected a *benab*—a shed made with sticks and branches—where he could spend the night. Pulling the dead animal close to him, he stretched out under this crude shelter and soon fell fast asleep.

But Kororomanna unknowingly built his benab near the road used by a group of unfriendly hebus. These particular hebus were forest spirits who were active only during the nights. Generally, they were very short with considerably hairy bodies and long, peculiar eyebrows—which jutted straight forward, making it difficult for them to look upward. To do so, they had to stand on their heads.

That night when Kororomanna built his benab, many of these hebus were traveling on the same road. As they hurried along to their various destinations, they became excessively noisy. Of course, the noise woke Kororomanna; and he, in turn, grew extremely angry with the hebus. To demonstrate this annoyance, he grabbed a huge stick and struck several times mightily at the dead monkey's body.

By then, the monkey's body had become greatly swollen. As Kororomanna hit it, it made a booming sound like a drum, and the loud sound quickly drew the hebus' attention. Almost at once, they searched carefully for the source and, shortly after, saw the dim shape of Kororomanna sitting under the benab.

Kororomanna strongly disliked the hebus. Additionally, he was always afraid of them, so he did not wait for them enter his benab. What he did was to quietly slip away into the darkness from the back of the benab and climb a tall *manicole* palm tree where he hid himself.

When the hebus entered the benab, they believed the big monkey lying on the ground was the one who made all the noise.

"You were very rude to disturb us with your noise," one of the hebus shouted.

With that, they all began to beat the dead animal mercilessly with sticks. It immediately sounded like a drum.

Meanwhile, Kororomanna, who was hiding among the branches of the manicole tree, became very amused with the sound of the swollen howler's body. It made him burst into uncontrollable laughter, and the hebus knew right away that something was wrong.

"This isn't the one who disturbed us," the leader said as he pointed at the dead animal. "This is a dead howler monkey. The one we're looking for is a man. He's up the manicole tree."

In a great rush, they all ran toward the manicole tree. And as they gathered around it, they stood on their heads with their feet in the air to see who was up in the tree.

"There he is!" they all shouted almost at once.

They saw Kororomanna still laughing, sitting among the tree branches.

"Let's cut down the tree," one of the hebus suggested to the others. With that, they immediately set to work with their axes. But since the axes were all made of turtle shells, they soon broke. The hebus then used their knives instead; but these were made of wood, and in no time, they also broke into pieces.

Finally, they decided to use a magic rope to pull Kororomanna down from the tree. The tip of this unusual magic rope was that of a live snake head. As soon as the rope reached Kororomanna, he quickly chopped off the head with his knife. As this happened, the rope instantly lost its magical power and fell limply to the ground.

The hebus then gathered under the tree to decide what they must do next. After much argument, one suggested, "Let's send the strongest of us up the tree to capture the man. As soon as he grabs the man, he must throw him down and shout, 'There is the man. Kill him quickly'."

They all agreed to this plan, and the strongest hebu clambered up the tree. But Kororomanna, who had heard their plans very clearly, was waiting for him. As soon as the hebu reached the branches, Kororomanna grabbed him and threw him down to the ground. "There is the man," Kororomanna shouted. "Kill him quickly!"

All the other hebus, who by this time had collected stout pieces of wood, began to mistakenly beat their friend, for it was too dark for them to see who it was.

While the beating was going on, Kororomanna quietly and cautiously glided down the tree trunk and soon escaped. It was not until the hebus had clubbed their friend to death that they realized what they had done.

Upon learning that they had been cleverly tricked by Kororomanna, they nonetheless continued their search for him. However, they were soon forced to abandon the search, for daylight began to slowly creep in and they were afraid of it.

The howler monkey

~ 23 ~

Kororomanna Escapes Again

After Kororomanna escaped from the manicole tree, he ran a good distance through the dense forest. But even though he escaped, he still feared that the hebus would continue to search for him. Desperately, he looked for a safe and secure hiding place; but because of the darkness, it was too difficult to find one, at first. Eventually, he came across a big hole located in a large tree trunk.

"This will certainly make a good hiding place," he said to himself. "I can remain inside this hollow tree trunk until daylight. In this way, I can escape easily because the hebus are afraid to move about in the daylight."

With that, he climbed into the hole. To his surprise, he found a young woman inside the tree.

"Who are you?" the frightened woman asked.

"I'm Kororomanna, the hunter. I'm hiding from the hebus, who are searching for me. What are you doing here?"

"This is my home," she stated. "My husband is a huge snake, a camudi, and we live here. You must leave at once. If you don't, he will eat you when he returns."

Despite this, Kororomanna was reluctant to leave. He was afraid the hebus would find and kill him. "I'm not afraid of a snake," he told her. "I'll stay here until the hebus give up their search."

The young woman begged him to go, but he insisted on staying.

Just as the sun rose, the snake returned from his nightly hunt. Immediately, he spotted Kororomanna sitting in a dark corner. He crawled up to him in a threatening manner.

"I'm going to eat you," he snarled.

At that very moment, a hummingbird flew past the hole on the tree trunk. Both Kororomanna and the snake saw it.

"That's my uncle," Kororomanna lied. "If you eat me, he will certainly kill you."

"You think I'm afraid of a little hummingbird?" the snake sneered.

Just as he spoke, a wild duck flew past.

"That's another of my uncles," Kororomanna told the snake. "If you eat me, he'll surely kill you."

"I'm not afraid of a wild duck," pointed out the snake.

Then a hawk flew past.

"That hawk is also my uncle," Kororomanna said. "If you eat me, he will certainly kill you."

The snake immediately became frightened, for it was a known fact that hawks loved to eat snakes, no matter how big they were.

"Look," he said, visibly frightened, "I won't eat you. But you have to leave right away."

Kororomanna, who was himself really afraid of the snake, slowly climbed out the hole without any further argument and continued his journey.

Since it was now daylight, he was not afraid of the hebus, but he was still lost in the forest. He walked until he found a narrow path. Though it was not familiar, he followed it for some time until he arrived at a place where a hollow tree trunk lay across the path. Peeking inside the trunk, he discovered a hebu child sitting there. Right away, Kororomanna became worried that the hebu child would tell the other hebus that he had passed that way. To prevent this from happening, he had no choice but to kill the child.

He was just about to continue his journey when he heard noises in the bushes nearby. He quickly climbed a tree and hid among its branches. As he settled himself among the branches, the hebu child's mother came out. She was frightened of the daylight, but when she saw her child was dead, she forgot about her fear and became very angry.

Just then, she saw Kororomanna's footprints near the trunk, but she could not follow them because there was no sandy soil off the path. Returning to her dead child, she scooped up the sand with one of Kororomanna's footprints and wrapped it in a large leaf. This she tied with a small vine and placed it near the hollow tree trunk and then set about collecting firewood in the bushes.

In the meantime, Kororomanna watched her closely from his hiding place, and he suspected that she was planning to hurt him by using magic. So the moment she moved away from the path into the tall bushes to look for more firewood, he swiftly climbed down the tree. Hurriedly, he untied the leaf containing the sand with his footprint. After throwing away the sand with his footprint, he substituted sand with the mother hebu's footprint. Upon completion of this task, he returned to his hiding place up the tree.

Shortly after, the mother hebu returned. She heaped the firewood she collected and got a big fire going. She then threw the leaf containing the footprint into the fire and shouted, "I curse the one whose footprint I burn. May he fall into the fire too."

But instead of Kororomanna, she found herself being pulled forcefully into the fire; and within a few minutes, she was burned to ashes.

The camudi (boa constrictor)

~ 24 ~

Further Adventures of Kororomanna

After outwitting the female hebu, Kororomanna continued his journey along the strange path. He followed it for hours until he eventually reached a wider, clearer track, which he felt would make his journey easier. However, this was not the case.

As soon as he stepped on the new path, his feet stuck fast to the ground. He tried hard to tug himself free, but the harder he tried, the more he became stuck.

"At last," sighed Kororomanna. "This is the end. I can't escape. This is a magical trap set by the hebus. I wonder how I can escape this."

He then threw himself on the ground and pretended to be dead—so much so that ants swarmed across him and stung him savagely, but he never moved. Actually, the clear path was a magical fish-and-animal trap set by the hebus who lived in the area. As night fell, a group of them came to see what they caught. When they saw Kororomanna stuck there, they thought they caught a large fish. They eagerly released Kororomanna from the magical trap and placed him on the ground near the path. All this time, he still pretended to be dead and remained limp.

"Let's take this large fish to the river and wash it," one hebu said. "See how it is covered with ants and dust?"

"We don't have a basket to fetch it," another said.

"Let's find some vines to make a basket," said the first one. "Then we can put the big fish inside and take it to the riverside."

All agreed, and they hurried off among the bushes to search for vines. With no one left to watch him, Kororomanna jumped up and ran away. But as he continued his wandering, he still could not find the pathway that led from the forest to his home.

Early the next morning, when it was still dark, he arrived at a clearing in which he saw a deep pond. On the bank was a hebu trying to empty the water with a little calabash bowl.

Kororomanna knew that if he was seen, his life would be in danger, so he decided to kill the hebu. He fired two arrows into the hebu's back, but the hebu did not seem to feel them. He thought they were flies and brushed them away with his hands.

When a third arrow struck him, he turned and saw Kororomanna who rushed toward the bushes to escape, only to trip on a vine and fall on his face.

In a flash, the hebu attacked him. He dragged Kororomanna near to the pond and imprisoned him in a hollow tree trunk.

"When I'm finished emptying water from the pond, I'll kill you," the hebu informed him.

Kororomanna was terrified. "Please don't kill me," he begged. "If you spare my life, I'll give you beautiful rattles."

"I don't want rattles," replied the hebu.

"I'll give you lots of paiwarri if you spare me," Kororomanna begged again.

"I don't want any paiwarri. I don't use any alcoholic drinks," declared the hebu. "Don't bother me. I'll kill you when I'm finished emptying the pond."

Kororomanna made a final plea. "Please don't kill me. I'll give you some tobacco if you set me free."

Since all hebus loved tobacco, he quickly released the hunter from the tree trunk.

"Where is the tobacco?" the hebu immediately demanded.

Luckily, Kororomanna had some in a little bag tied to his belt. He handed it to his captor, who was delighted by such a valuable gift. He chewed some for a while, then declared, "You're the first man to give me tobacco. From now on, we will be friends."

"I prefer to be your friend instead of your enemy," replied Kororomanna.

"What's your name?" asked the hebu.

"My name is Kororomanna. What's yours?"

"I'm Huta Kurakura."

"Why are you emptying the pond?" Kororomanna asked.

"This pond has a lot of fish. It will be easier to catch them without the water," explained Huta Kurakura.

So Kororomanna helped him empty the water in the pond. Later, they both collected the large amount of fish, which Huta Kurakura divided into two heaps.

"One is yours," he told Kororomanna.

Kororomanna pointed out, "I won't be able to take so many fish home."

"That's no problem," his hebu friend replied.

He used his magic to tie Kororomanna's share in a small leaf-covered bundle.

"All your fish are in here," he explained. "Follow the path that leads away from the pond and you'll find your way home."

After saying farewell to Huta Kurakura, Kororomanna picked up his tiny bundle and followed the pathway. Eventually, he discovered he was on a familiar trail that would lead him to his home.

Finally, he arrived home where his wife and mother were wondering what happened to him since he had been missing for a while. They were indeed very happy to see him once again.

After he told them of his adventures, he showed them the little bundle.

"I brought a lot of fish for you," he stated with a little grin.

The two women laughed loudly when they saw the little bundle.

"How could such a tiny thing hold a lot of fish?" his mother asked in disbelief.

With that, Kororomanna untied the tiny bundle. So many fish came out of it that the house was filled from the floor to the roof. Kororomanna, his wife, and his mother had to rush outside instantly since there was no space left to accommodate them.

After their excitement subsided, they invited all the people of the village to take as many fish as they needed. Finally, they managed to get back into their house. And for a few weeks that followed, fish was the main meal for all the people of Kororomanna's village.

A tobacco plant

~ 25 ~

The Origin of the Calabash

The Arawak people enjoyed long periods of happiness in the past, but there were times when they endured great sufferings as well. There was one particular period when all bad things seemed to happen especially to them.

This was a time of heavy incessant rainfall, which lasted for several weeks. Rivers overflowed and flooded the countryside, and soon, even the soil of the farmlands was washed away.

Then, all of a sudden, the rain stopped—but not without destroying all the crops in the land. As such, very little food was available for the people. Further, all the animals the Arawaks usually hunted had moved deeper into the forest to the distant mountains where they had escaped the rising waters. Still, the Arawaks did not give up. They decided to plant crops once again; but since most of the soil nutrients were washed away in the flood, the plants did not survive too long.

As a result, a great famine engulfed the entire land. Hunger became rampant, and countless illnesses affected the people. Not a single day went by without the Arawaks mourning the deaths of children, young adults, and the elderly. While women wailed over the deaths of loved ones, men silently wondered how the times of abundant food and no disease could ever return.

During that same period, among the Arawaks, was a piaman named Arawanili. Not happy with what was happening in his land, he used his charms and magical powers in an effort to drive away the suffering. But all this he did to no avail.

Due to this failure, the people rebuked him.

"You're no longer a worthy piaman," they told him. "Your charms and magic are weak. We don't need you if you can't help us."

Despite these insults, Arawanili was still genuinely sad to see his people suffer. He fully understood why everyone was so terribly angry with him. Surely, they rejected him out of frustration, but he was even more dejected when he saw the hopelessness in their eyes.

Early one morning, as Arawanili sat on the riverbank, numerous thoughts began to swirl around in his head. He thought of the hardships his people endured, of the deaths of children and adults, and of the difficulty he was having by not being able to use his magical powers. And as he sat there and gazed at the river's still waters, a female water spirit suddenly arose. Arawanili became instantly dumbfounded.

"Don't be afraid, Arawanili," the water spirit encouraged him. "My name is Orehu. I came here to help you assist your people overcome their misery and suffering."

"But they have already rejected me," replied Arawanili sadly. "They say that I'm not a worthy piaman anymore."

"You see, they are frustrated by all their suffering," Orehu responded. "They aren't responsible for their words."

"How can I help stop the misery and suffering we face?" the piaman inquired.

"Let me explain," Orehu pointed out. "Your magic, like that of all piamen, is weak against the evil spirits that bring famine and disease to the people. You need something more powerful to use against those spirits."

Having said that, Orehu pulled a branch bearing light-green leaves from under the water. She handed it to Arawanili, saying, "Plant this. When it bears fruits, pick two and meet me at this place. Only then will I be able to show you how to help your people. I'll be waiting for you."

Orehu then gently dived under the water and disappeared.

Arawanili took the precious branch home and planted it in his yard. After many months, it grew into a small shady tree, and it soon bore large green gourds.

One morning, as promised, he picked two gourds and went down to the riverbank to meet Orehu. As soon as he sat down, the water spirit rose from the water and climbed up the bank to sit beside him. She gently took the gourds from him and carefully examined them.

"This gourd is known as calabash," she explained. "It will be very useful to the people. The outer skin becomes a hard shell. After the soft inner parts are removed, the calabash can be made into bowls, water containers, and other useful things."

With that, Orehu cut one of the gourds into halves with a sharp knife. She then scraped off the soft white kernel and made two neat bowls. Then she took the other gourd and bored two holes in it, one at the top and the other at the bottom. Through those holes, she removed the inner kernel until the gourd became hollow. She placed a few white pebbles in the hollow gourd then put a stick through the holes, leaving part of the stick extended for a handle. After its completion, she grasped the handle and shook the gourd, which made a rattling sound.

"This is a *maraca*," she said. "You can make it even more beautiful by tying feathers to the handle. When you shake it, the rattling sound will chase away the evil spirits that are bringing suffering to your people."

She handed him the maraca and watched as he shook it.

"Shake the maraca whenever you practice your charms," Orehu said. "Good times will certainly come again."

She gave Arawanili a last reminder: "Remember to always use the calabash properly. No part must be wasted. Even the kernel that is dug out from it can be used for curing sores and cuts. Rub the kernel on the affected parts of the body."

Then Orehu dived into the river and disappeared.

Arawanili returned home and began to practice his charms once again. This time, he used his maraca to make loud rattling sounds that chased away the evil spirits.

Surprisingly, the crops in the land started to grow again, and the sick people fully regained their strength. Once again, happiness reigned over the entire land.

Since then, the calabash, no doubt, became one of the most useful possessions of the people. They used it for making bowls, water containers, and maracas. But at first, maracas were used only by the piamen. Later, as musicians eventually adopted it, the maracas became popular musical instruments.

The calabash tree with gourds

Calabash bowls

~ 26 ~

How Birds Got Their Plumage

Once upon a time, there was a huge water snake living in a small lake in the forest. It was a huge creature with a most brilliant skin of red, yellow, green, black, and white in extraordinary patterns.

Since the snake hunted small animals and birds for his meals, he became such a terror to all other living creatures that the men and all the small animals and birds, who were friends in those days, combined forces to destroy him.

From time to time, the men in the area tried to capture it to obtain its colorful skin. However, it eluded all the traps that they set. But the men were very much afraid of the snake and dared not enter the lake. Eventually, they all decided that anyone who killed the snake would be given its skin.

But the other animals in the area were also afraid of this snake because, in the night, he slipped out from the lake and ate small animals and birds that nested on the ground. Eventually, even the birds decided that they would have to make an effort to kill the snake.

But all of them were afraid to tackle him except the gray heron who circled the lake armed with his bow and arrows. Then one day as the snake lifted himself above the water, the heron shot an arrow through his head and killed him instantly. The heron quickly called the other birds to help him pull the dead snake to the side of the lake.

Immediately, all the men in the area ran out of their homes to see the dead snake. They hurriedly skinned it, and as they were about to take its precious skin away, the heron strongly objected.

"Since you did not kill the snake, you have no right to take its skin," he argued.

The leader of the men then consulted with the others and finally told the heron, "If you can carry away the skin, we will allow you to have it."

109

The men thought that since the skin was very large and heavy, the little gray heron would be unable to lift it.

But the heron, in bird language, asked all the other birds for help. Together, they grabbed the colorful skin by their beaks and flew away with it.

Eventually, they arrived at a place where no humans lived; and when they landed on the ground, they admired the skin with its many beautiful colors.

"What will we do with this beautiful skin?" asked the parrot.

"Well, I think that since all of us brought it to this place, we must each take a piece of it," suggested the heron.

They all agreed to this suggestion, and as each bird took a piece of the skin, its feathers automatically changed to the color of the piece it collected.

So parrots became green or red, macaws became red or yellow, *sakis* turned blue, and flamingos became red. Some birds also acquired more than one color since the portion of skin they collected had specks of other hues. Thus, guinea birds became gray with white spots, kiskadees became yellow and black, and woodpeckers turned brown and gray.

The heron, though, collected the skin taken from the snake's head (which was gray), so the hue of his feathers did not change.

"Bright colors would make men shoot arrows at me," he explained. "By being gray, they would not see me easily."

The kiskadee

The guinea bird

~ 27 ~

Tiger's Shining Yellow Eyes

One day as Tiger was walking by the seaside, he saw a little distance away a crab throwing some small round objects into the sea, which soon after would jump out from the water and return to him.

As Tiger moved closer, to his surprise, he noticed that the crab was actually removing his eyes and throwing them into the sea.

"What are you doing, my brother?" Tiger asked in great dismay.

"Oh, I am just playing with my eyes," the crab replied.

"Well, you seem to be having quite a good time," said Tiger. "Show me how you do it."

But the crab was not willing to do this.

"Look here, Tiger," he said, "I can't make you play this game with your eyes because a big shark lives in the sea."

Nevertheless, Tiger insisted, and finally, the crab agreed to show him how the game was played. As Tiger looked on, the crab removed his eyes and threw them into the sea while singing softly, "Go, my eyes, go to the middle of the sea. Go, go, go!"

Now to retrieve his eyes, he began to sing this other tune: "My eyes, from the middle of the sea, come back to me, come back to me."

And immediately, the crab's eyes leaped out of the water and returned into their sockets.

Tiger was amazed, and he shouted excitedly, "I want to play this game! Remove my eyes and throw them in the sea as you did with yours."

But the crab discouraged him.

"I can't let you play this game," he told Tiger, "because a big shark swims in the sea, and he may eat up your eyes."

But Tiger was eager to play this game. After continuous pleadings, the crab finally agreed. He touched Tiger's eyes while singing loudly, "Go, eyes of Tiger, go to the middle of the sea. Go, go, go!"

And Tiger's eyes leaped out of his head and flew into the sea.

Without sight and surrounded by total darkness, Tiger immediately became very frightened, and he jumped about and roared loudly.

"Bring back my eyes! Crab, bring back my eyes!" he roared angrily.

But there was no response from the crab, so the extremely scared Tiger tried on his own to get back his eyes by screaming out loudly, "My eyes, from the middle of the sea, come back to me, come back to me!"

However, nothing happened. His eyes remained at the bottom of the sea.

With a feeling of terror, Tiger became even more afraid, and jumped and roared louder and louder. Then the crab spoke quietly to him, "It is because you are screaming and roaring that your eyes refuse to obey you."

Tiger immediately stopped roaring. "Please, my brother, help me get back my eyes," he begged the crab.

Then the crab sang sweetly, "Eyes of my brother, from the middle of the sea, come back to him, come back to him."

And the eyes immediately returned to Tiger's face, and his sight was restored.

As this was done, the crab advised, "Now take care of your eyes. If you play this game, the big shark in the sea could swallow them."

Naturally, Tiger was most happy to regain his eyes, and he felt that he had become alarmed too quickly when his eyes were in the sea. So he felt that he must play the game once more.

He begged the crab to have his eyes thrown into the sea once again, but to no avail. But when his continued pleas finally got on the crab's nerves, he finally decided to do what Tiger wanted.

So the crab sang loudly, "Go, eyes of Tiger, go to the middle of the sea. Go, go, go!"

Tiger's eyes jumped out and again flew into the sea.

But just then, the big shark was swimming in the area, and he swallowed them as they sank to the bottom.

Of course, neither Tiger nor the crab knew of this, so they were not alarmed. Tiger himself was more relaxed this time and was not afraid of his blindness. After a little while, he said to the crab, "Please call back my eyes."

So the crab sang sweetly, "Eyes of my brother, from the middle of the sea, come back to him, come back to him."

But this time, the eyes did not return!

So the crab sang out once more, but still the eyes failed to come back.

The blind Tiger, now aware that something had gone dreadfully wrong, also sang sweetly, "My eyes, from the middle of the sea, come back to me, come back to me."

But his eyes failed to come back.

"Where are my eyes?" he roared in anger.

"I warned you not to play this game," replied the crab. "It's possible that the big shark swallowed them."

That made Tiger even angrier, and he jumped and roared and blindly tried to hit the crab. But the crab managed to keep away from him and finally crawled into the sea to escape.

So the lonely, blind Tiger remained on the beach for many days. Because he could not run, he could not hunt, and so he began to starve. He was dying of hunger when the piaman of the area found him stretched out near to some bushes.

"What happened to you?" inquired the piaman. "You look as if you are starving."

"I'm very ill," groaned Tiger. "I'm blind and hungry because the crab caused my eyes to jump into the middle of the sea, and they never came back."

"You really look very ill," observed the piaman.

"Please help me," begged Tiger. "When I recover, I will hunt deer for you."

Feeling sorry for him, the piaman told him, "Stay here while I go and search for some medicine."

He then looked for a briar bush and collected the yellow gum on its stems and returned to the seaside where Tiger was waiting. He built a fire and melted the gum into a thick liquid in a small pot.

"What are you doing?" asked Tiger impatiently.

"Have a little patience," replied the piaman.

When the molten gum was ready, the piaman ordered Tiger to bow his head. He then drained the molten gum into Tiger's empty eye sockets, one after the other. At first, Tiger did not feel anything, but when he straightened himself, he screamed in pain. And he rolled on the sand and roared loudly.

"Why is someone as strong and fierce as you roaring so much?" asked the piaman.

"It is because my eyes are burning badly," Tiger responded.

"Then you must open them so that the breeze will cool them," directed the piaman.

Carefully, Tiger opened his eyes, and at first everything seemed to be yellow in color. Gradually, his eyesight returned; and when he looked into a nearby pool of clear seawater, he noticed that he had clear, shining yellow eyes.

"You can go now to hunt deer for me," the piaman ordered.

And ever since that time, Tiger continued to hunt deer for the piaman to repay him for those shining yellow eyes.

The jaguar (the Guyanese "tiger")

~ 28 ~

Koneso and the Village Chief

Koneso was a mischievous rabbit who possessed some magical powers, which enabled him to appear as a young man from time to time. He had very short ears and could run very fast. But everywhere he went, he caused much mischief and outwitted many people as well as other animals. Because of this trait, he acquired many enemies. But his magical powers saved him from the growing numbers of enemies. If anyone aimed at him with a club or an arrow, it would either glide off or break, and Koneso would jeeringly laugh at them as he made his escape. He, therefore, continued his mischief, thus causing much annoyance to all.

After a while, Koneso became tired of the area where he lived, and much to the delight of everyone there, he departed for another place far away. When he eventually arrived at the new village, he discovered that it was ruled by a powerful chief who had the most beautiful daughter.

When Koneso saw the lovely woman one day, he swore that he must have her as his wife. So he brazenly approached the chief and said, "My name is Koneso, and I want to marry your daughter."

The chief looked at him with much surprise and laughed. But shortly thereafter, he spoke to him, "Before I can agree to give you my daughter, you must first bring me two quakes full of alligator and camudi eyes."

The chief certainly did not like Koneso, so he set this impossible task, which he was sure Koneso could never accomplish.

But Koneso, without wasting much time, set out for the riverside where he cut some bamboo and began to weave the two quakes. At the same time, he brewed a large quantity of casiri, which he filled in many jugs.

Then early one morning, he brought the filled jugs to the riverbank and put them under some shady trees. He then took a comfortable seat and began playing some wonderful tunes on his bone flute.

The music was so soothing and captivating that all the alligators and camudis came out of the water and listened attentively.

And as they became so mesmerized with this wonderful music, Koneso served them each a calabash with casiri.

Not long after, they were all intoxicated with the casiri, and soon, they fell fast asleep. So, without wasting any time, Koneso hurriedly dug out all their eyes and packed his quakes.

With his two quakes full of eyes, he rushed to the chief's house.

"Here are the quakes with the eyes," he said as the chief looked at the collection in disbelief. "Now you must keep your promise and let me marry your daughter."

But the chief was not prepared to agree to his promise. In rage he shouted, "I can't let an insolent one as you have my daughter."

And with much anger, he grabbed Koneso's ears and pulled mightily. Koneso's ears stretched to his shoulders, and to this day, they remain like that on all rabbits.

Koneso, undoubtedly, was very angry with the chief for breaking his promise and also for physically deforming him. In disgrace, he left the chief's house, all the while thinking of how he could take his revenge. As he walked through the village, everyone laughed and jeered at his long ears, and this made him even angrier.

Still, he was determined to win the chief's daughter, so whenever he saw her, he would attempt to speak to her.

But the chief instructed his servants to guard her and not let him get close to her.

However, he persisted, so they reported to the chief, who instructed, "Whenever you see him, give him a sound beating."

So the next time, the guards surrounded Koneso and lashed out at him with long heavy sticks. But none of these sticks hit him, for they all broke into pieces before they made contact with his skin.

When the chief learnt that Koneso could not be hurt by being beaten, he told the guards, "The next time you see him, grab him and tie him up against a tree and shoot him with your arrows at close range. I want him dead."

And as Koneso walked through the village the very next day, the guards quickly grabbed and tied him against a tree. As they shot arrows at him, the arrows broke into pieces as soon as they came close to Koneso's skin.

Again, the guards reported their failure to the chief, who flew into a terrible rage and yelled, "This time, tie him up in a canoe and set him adrift in the sea."

Obeying the chief's instructions, the guards then tied him up tightly and took him to the seaside. There, they threw him into a canoe and pushed it out to sea. As the current pulled the canoe away from land, Koneso, using his magic powers, released himself and turned the vessel back toward the shore.

That same afternoon, Koneso brazenly walked into the chief's house and told him, "I have brought back your canoe safely."

The chief shouted for his men, "Seize him! Bind his hands and feet together, tie a heavy stone to his neck, and throw him into the sea this time."

With that, the guards did as the chief told them and took Koneso out into the deep sea and dumped him overboard. With the heavy stone around his neck, he quickly sank to the bottom.

Once again, his magic powers saved him, and he was able to free himself. Lifting the heavy stone on his shoulder, he walked along the seabed to the shore. And late that afternoon, carrying the heavy stone on his shoulder, he went to the chief's house. To the astounded chief and his guards, he declared, "I have brought back your stone safely."

The chief knew he could do nothing more to get rid of Koneso.

"You have won," he told him. "Your powers are exceptionally great, so I will keep my promise. You can have my daughter as your wife."

The rabbit

~ 29 ~

Koneso and Tiger

After a while, Koneso decided that he wanted to visit his old village where he grew up. On his way, he had to pass through a thick forest, but he could not help playing his old tricks once again—this time on Tiger, who lived in that same part of the forest.

So he began to make plans to outsmart Tiger. Intertwined on the tall trees were some thick rope vines, which he began to pull noisily so as to draw Tiger's attention. He succeeded shortly thereafter, for Tiger heard the commotion and decided to investigate. There he saw Koneso tugging at the thick vines.

"What's all this noise about?" Tiger questioned.

"Oh, it's really nothing," Koneso replied seriously. "But a heavy wind will begin to blow the day after tomorrow, and since I don't want to be blown away, I plan to tie myself to a big tree with these vines."

Upon hearing this information, Tiger became quite alarmed.

"I don't want to be blown away either," he said.

"Then, my brother, you should try and do something to save yourself," advised Koneso.

"Please tie me to a tree before you tie yourself," pleaded Tiger.

"All right," replied Koneso. "Let's find a big tree to which I can tie you."

Tiger soon found a strong tree and allowed Koneso to tie him tightly against it with the vines he had pulled down. Then Koneso went about pulling down and cutting away at more vines, all the time making as much noise as he could to give the impression that he was gathering enough vines to tie up himself also.

But as soon as he was out of Tiger's sight, he quietly slipped away, leaving the helpless Tiger strapped tightly against the tree.

Meanwhile, two days went by but no heavy wind came, so Tiger called out to Koneso. There was no answer. He called again and again but still got no answer. The wily rabbit had tricked him for sure, he soon realized.

With two whole days tied to the tree without food or water, Tiger became excessively hungry, so he tried desperately to free himself. He pulled and tugged at the ropes, but they were so securely fastened that he found it difficult to get loose. After much frustration, he became highly annoyed and roared loudly.

From time to time, as other forest animals passed by, he pleaded with them to set him free. But they all looked at him suspiciously and walked away, for they knew that if he was set free, he would surely eat them up. Even the fierce and powerful harpy eagle, flying by, ignored his appeals.

But help came at last when Carrion-Crow arrived on the fourth day.

"Brother Carrion-Crow, please untie me from this tree," Tiger begged him. "I promise that if you untie these ropes, I will always, in the future, give you some meat to eat."

Since meat was such an important part of Carrion-Crow's diet, he quickly began to untie the tight knots on the ropes binding Tiger to the tree.

Tiger was so pleased that, ever since that day, whenever he killed an animal, he would always leave some meat on the carcass for Carrion-Crow.

As was expected, Tiger wanted to find Koneso quickly to punish him for the trick he played on him; for by this time, all the forest animals had learned how this clever rabbit had outsmarted him. So he sought information from other animals as to the whereabouts of the trickster. Eventually, he learned of a pond where Koneso would bathe from time to time. So he hid in the branches of an overhanging tree near the pond.

But Tiger had to wait there for quite a while since Koneso did not have a fixed time for his bath. Eventually, Tiger spotted someone coming along the track leading to the pond. But Tiger was uncertain who it was. Actually, it was Koneso coming from a party, but because he was covered with flower garlands, it was difficult for Tiger to recognize him.

But as he entered the pond, he looked up and spotted Tiger in the tree. Swiftly, Tiger sprang at Koneso, but the rabbit dashed away from the pond with Tiger in hot pursuit. They both raced down the forest track, and just as Tiger was about to grab hold of him, Koneso plunged into an armadillo hole. Since the hole was too small for Tiger to enter, he decided to fill it up with dirt to bury Koneso alive. But there was no digging stick nearby, and he did not trust to move away from the hole since the rabbit may escape.

Then he looked around and saw a female hawk sitting on a tree nearby.

"Hey there, Sister Hawk," he called out.

"Hey there, Tiger," the hawk responded.

"Please do me a favor and guard this armadillo hole," Tiger told the hawk. "Koneso, the trickster rabbit, is hiding in it, and I have to search for a digging stick to fill this hole."

Now the hawk herself had been tricked by Koneso in the past, so she was happy that the trickster was now cornered.

"All right," the hawk said. "I'll stand by the hole."

With that, the hawk flew down and stood by the hole as Tiger went into the bushes in search of a stick.

While in the hole, Koneso overheard their conversation and, peeping out, he saw the hawk standing guard nearby. So he called out sweetly to her, "Why does a pretty bird like you have to obey Tiger?"

The vain hawk was extremely flattered by Koneso's sweet words.

"Do you think I'm pretty?" she asked.

"You are indeed a very beautiful bird with your smooth, soft feathers," Koneso replied. "Come and bend your face over this hole so I can see how truly beautiful you are."

With that, the hawk strutted to the hole to show her face. Immediately, Koneso threw a handful of sand into her eyes, thus temporarily blinding her, and this gave him the chance to quickly escape from the hole and from the rage of Tiger.

The harpy eagle

~ 30 ~

Konehu Holds Up the Mountain

Konehu was, indeed, the laziest man in the entire region, and he made little effort to do any sort of work. As a result, he was always without food, but his ability to play tricks on others enabled him to survive from day to day.

One afternoon as he was sitting idly at the foot of a high overhanging cliff on the mountainside, he felt very hungry and wondered how he could manage to find something to eat. Just then, he saw three men walking along the path near the cliff. The men, who were hunters from the nearby village, were fetching some deer and bush-hogs that they had killed during the hunt.

Without any hesitation, Konehu grabbed a long wooden pole and pushed it against the side of the cliff as if it was a brace. As the hunters approached, he pressed against it, grunting all the time as if he was exhausted.

The men looked at him in astonishment.

"Why are you bracing so hard against the pole?" one of them asked.

"Don't you see the mountain is falling over?" Konehu grunted. "If I don't brace it up with this pole, it will tumble and destroy the village."

The hunters, upon hearing this news, seemed quite shocked.

"Look up and you can see how the mountain is moving!" Konehu said, looking up as he leaned heavily on the pole. "Look here. The three of you should now brace on the pole and allow me to rest a little. I have been bracing it all day."

The three hunters then looked up the steep cliff and saw the clouds moving over it.

"Yes, indeed, the mountain looks as if it is falling!" one of them exclaimed in alarm.

"Let us help brace it up!" another shouted.

They shoved their collection of deer and hogs under some bushes and then stood in place to brace the mountain. As they did so, Konehu slowly wandered away into the shady bushes.

The hunters pressed harder and harder against the heavy pole until late in the afternoon when the sun was sinking behind the mountain. By this time, they were terribly exhausted and felt they could continue no longer.

"How much longer can we brace this mountain?" one of them queried. "Certainly, if it falls, it won't be our fault."

And with that, they left the pole in place and moved to the bushes to collect their game. But everything had disappeared! They began searching around for Konehu, but he too was nowhere in sight.

Only then did it dawn on them that they were truly outsmarted by the sly Konehu. So they sadly made their way home after losing all their precious game to Konehu.

Bush-hogs (peccary)

~ 31 ~

Konehu and the Tigress

One day, while the cunning Konehu was walking along a forest path, he met a tigress with three little cubs.

"What are you doing here?" he asked.

"I'm waiting here for someone to help me take care of my cubs," the tigress replied. "I want to go hunting, but I can't leave them all alone."

"I will be happy to look after them for you," offered Konehu.

So the tigress left her cubs with Konehu and went into the forest to hunt. When she returned in the evening, she thanked Konehu and shared some of the meat she had gathered. She then suckled her cubs, one after the other.

Konehu was quite happy with this arrangement since he did not have to perform any serious physical labor to obtain his food supply. As a result, he assisted the tigress every day with her cubs while she went off hunting.

So to keep a close eye on the cubs, Konehu kept them in a large hollow log, which was very cool and comfortable during the hot day. Everything went well for him, and he was quite satisfied. But one day, one of the cubs bit him, and he became so annoyed that he hit the cub on its head, killing it instantly. He hurriedly disposed of the body by burying it some distance away.

When the tigress returned in the evening, Konehu pretended as if nothing had happened.

"Bring me my babies to suckle," she told Konehu.

Without any worry at all, Konehu brought one cub after another from the hollow log to their mother, but this time he brought one of them twice. And since the cubs all looked alike, the tigress had no clue that one was missing.

Then on the next day, another cub bit Konehu. This time, he immediately killed it and disposed of the body as before. Again, he said nothing to the mother when she came home that evening and brought out the only cub left three times to be suckled, without the mother realizing that it was the same cub.

Then the following day, the last cub bit Konehu on his arm and, in a terrible rage, he killed it. But this time, he knew he could not remain there for the tigress's return, so he left the dead cub near the hollow log and ran away. He ran on and on until he became very tired, and after taking a short rest, he continued his long run again. He was sure that the tigress would eventually follow him, so he wanted to move as far away as possible.

At last, he reached a place far away in the savannah where he decided to build a house. His house stood on very tall posts, and access could only be gained by climbing up a long ladder. When the framework of the house was completed, he set about collecting *troolie* palm leaves to thatch the roof.

Meanwhile, when the tigress returned home that day and found the dead cub near the hollow log, she called out for Konehu. Upon hearing no answer, she looked around for her other cubs.

In a rage, she roared loudly, "Konehu killed my cubs! I'll find him and kill him!"

With no delay whatsoever, she immediately left in search of Konehu. She thoroughly searched the forest that night and throughout the following day but could find him nowhere.

Then she moved into the savannah to continue the search. Finally, she arrived at the place where Konehu was building his house. At the time, he was very busy thatching the roof.

"Konehu!" she shouted. "You killed my cubs! I will kill you!"

But strangely, Konehu showed no sign of fear.

From his high perch, he shouted down to the tigress, "You'd better try to save yourself."

"Why should I try to save myself?" she growled.

"Because the sea is rising, and when the water reaches here, you'll be drowned," he shouted back. "I'm building this tall house to save myself."

As she looked at the tall posts of his house, she became less angry and more worried.

"What should I do to save myself?" she asked.

"Well, why don't you climb up the ladder and join me?" Konehu replied. "The seawater will not reach us up here."

Gladly, the tigress climbed up the ladder to the house while Konehu was still sitting on the rafters, tying thatch to the roof. But he felt somewhat threatened when he saw her climbing to reach the rafters.

Suddenly he said, "Oh my, I have to go downstairs to get more string to tie the thatch. Wait here. I'll be back shortly."

But as soon as he touched the ground, he removed the ladder, leaving the tigress helpless in the high house.

Then he raced away from the area.

When the tigress spotted him escaping, she roared, "You tricked me! I will catch you and eat you."

Konehu kept running for many days. Intermittently, he rested and then ran again until he reached another forest area. This time, he cut some bamboo then seated himself on the limb of a *mora* tree and started to make a quake with the pieces of bamboo.

Meanwhile, back at the tall house, the tigress felt trapped, for she could not climb down because the ladder was gone. She feared leaping to the ground since the height was too great and she might just kill herself.

She was surely trapped there, and after an entire day passed, she became very hungry and thirsty. Eventually, it dawned on her that she would have to make an effort to escape or else she would starve to death. After some serious thinking, she made up her mind to make the leap to the ground even if she had to risk her life. So she closed her eyes and jumped and landed with a heavy, painful thump on the ground. She felt as if all her bones were broken, but thankfully, she was still alive. Then she slowly lifted herself on her feet and managed to reach a nearby stream where she quenched her unbearable thirst.

She was extremely angry with Konehu. With gnashing teeth, she grumbled, "I'll kill that evil Konehu."

After walking for one night and day, she spotted Konehu as he sat on the mora tree making his quake.

"Good! I've trapped you here," she roared at him. "I definitely will kill you and eat you for my dinner."

But Konehu showed no fear.

"I think you'd better try to save yourself," he shouted down to her.

"Why must I save myself?" she shouted back.

Then Konehu told her: "Remember I told you that the seawater is rising and is coming this way? Well, it is still coming. That is the reason I'm making this quake. When it is completed, I will get inside and pull myself to the uppermost branch of this big mora tree where the water will not reach me. If you don't believe me, then you can remain down there and get drowned."

Again, the gullible tigress believed him and became very frightened.

"Please put me in the quake," she begged. "I don't want to be drowned."

"Well, you have to wait for a while because I have to make the quake bigger," said Konehu.

So Konehu increased the size of the quake as the tigress waited in great anxiety under the tree. When the job was completed, he tied a long rope vine to it and let it down to the ground.

"Climb inside," he instructed the tigress.

She quickly clambered inside, and Konehu swiftly slid down the tree and tightly tied up the quake cover, imprisoning the tigress. Then he threw the loose end of the long rope vine to the uppermost branch of the tree and pulled the quake upward until it was suspended high above the ground.

Laughing loudly, Konehu ran away from the area. As she watched him running away, the tigress once again knew she had been tricked. She roared loudly in her prison and called for help, but since the other animals feared her, they all ran away too.

The tigress was now in a bad position, for as she continued to roar, all the other animals kept on running away from the area. But a curious monkey wanted to know why the tigress was locked up in the quake, so he climbed down the rope vine and untied the cover. In an instant, the tigress sprang out of the quake and she and the monkey fell heavily to the ground. The enraged tigress, instead of thanking her savior, immediately killed him and ravenously devoured him. Then without giving up, she set out to find Konehu. She vowed that she would not allow herself to be tricked again this time and was absolutely sure that she would kill her tormentor on meeting him again.

For many days she trailed Konehu until she saw him on the bank of a small river. When he saw her approaching, Konehu stared intently into the river as if he was studying something in the water.

"There you are!" shouted the tigress. "This time, I'll kill you and eat you for my dinner."

But Konehu seemed unafraid and continued staring intently into the water.

The inquisitive tigress wondered why he was behaving that way. "What are you looking at?" she asked.

"Look quickly down there," he replied, pointing into the water. "Don't you see a big round rock of gold? If you get that, you will become very rich."

The silly tigress looked into the still water and, indeed, saw far below what looked like a big round rock of gold.

But actually, it was only the reflection of the sun overhead, but the greedy tigress was sure that it was a big lump of gold on the riverbed.

In a flash, she dived into the river, but unable to hold her breath for too long, she rose to the surface to breathe.

"You have to go deeper," Konehu instructed.

She took a deep breath and dived down but soon came up again to breathe.

Again Konehu said, "You have to go even deeper to get the gold."

And so the tigress continued diving and coming up to breathe, with Konehu instructing her to dive deeper and deeper into the river. Finally, when she made another dive and remained longer than before under the water, Konehu seized the opportunity to escape into the nearby forest.

When the tigress surfaced, she could not see Konehu. She became very angry with herself, for she knew he had tricked her again. After resting for a while, she again set about searching for her tormentor. For many days she wandered over the forests, mountains, and savannahs until, at last, she saw him on top of a mountain. He was holding on to a big round rock as she stared up at him.

"Now that I've found you, I will not let you escape," she said. "I will certainly kill you this time."

As she spoke, Konehu wrapped his arms around the big round rock, which stood on the edge of a pit.

"What are you holding on to?" she asked.

"Oh, this is a large piece of meat which is too much for me," he replied. "If you come up, I can give it to you."

The greedy tigress was excited about receiving a big chunk of meat. So she raced up the mountainside, and as she reached the pit, Konehu pushed the rock forward. It rolled down and smashed the tigress, killing her instantly.

And that was how Konehu finally got rid of the tigress.

Jaguar cubs

~ 32 ~

Konehu and His Wonderful Bird

Konehu's tricks became well-known all over the region, and people refused to give him any food unless he worked for it. But even when he did some work, he always found a way to cheat.

One morning, looking hungry and weary, he showed up at a farmer's house.

"Can you give me something to eat?" he begged the farmer.

"You are a lazy good-for-nothing," the farmer rebuked him. "I won't give you any food unless you do some work for me."

The lazy Konehu had no alternative but to do the work.

So, shortly thereafter, the farmer brought a quantity of *paddy* and a wooden *mortar*.

"You must pound this paddy in the mortar, then sift it and collect the rice," the farmer instructed.

"All right," Konehu answered. "But I will use my own mortar stick to pound the paddy."

"Do as you like," the farmer told him, "but make certain you gather some clean rice at the end, or I won't give you anything."

Having delivered his orders, the farmer went about his own task while Konehu was left to complete his.

And later that afternoon, when the farmer went to collect the cleaned rice, he was surprised at seeing only a small amount.

"How is it you have this small quantity of rice from the big heap of paddy I gave you?" the farmer questioned.

"Well, I don't know," replied Konehu. "I pounded the paddy, and this is the amount of rice I got."

So the next day, the farmer gave Konehu the same quantity of paddy, and when he checked back later, he received an even smaller quantity of rice than the previous day.

"Look here, Konehu," the farmer said angrily. "I'll pay you for your labor, but don't ever come back because I'm not satisfied with the amount of rice you are giving me."

Smiling slyly, Konehu grabbed his heavy mortar stick and hurried home. That night, he enjoyed a hearty meal of cooked rice for his dinner.

But how did he manage to get the rice?

Instead of a solid heavy-wood mortar stick to pound the paddy, Konehu had used a big hollow bamboo; so while he was shelling the paddy, he cleverly filled up the bamboo pounder with rice.

After a while, Konehu became very notorious for pulling tricks on people in far-off regions as well. When this news reached a very rich chief in a village very far away, he bragged that the trickster could never get the advantage of him.

The chief had a big farm, a large house, and a spacious storehouse loaded with corn, yams, sweet potatoes, and cassava. And since he knew the history of his people well and could read the stars and predict the weather, all the villagers held him in high esteem.

"No one can ever trick me," bragged the chief as he was told of Konehu's exploits.

But not long after, Konehu heard of this wealthy chief, so he decided to visit his village. When he arrived there, he dressed himself in tattered clothes and went straight to the chief's farmland where he dug a small hole and covered it with the leaves of a troolie palm.

After staying there for a while, he spotted the chief approaching with his bow and arrows, so he immediately pressed down on the palm leaves pretending he had trapped an animal.

The chief noticed this strange man in ragged clothing pressing down on the palm leaves and asked, "What are you doing there?"

Konehu looked up to him. "I caught a wonderful bird in this hole," he said, "but I'm afraid it will fly away. Do you have a quake to use as a cage?"

Not knowing who the man was, nor suspecting any trickery, he replied, "No, I don't have one here, but if you go to my house, you will find a few hanging on posts at the back."

"But you will have to hold down these leaves to prevent the bird from escaping," Konehu said to him.

So the chief decided to help out this poor, strange man and pressed down on the palm leaves.

Konehu hurried away to the large house where he met the chief's wife who was just about to leave for market.

"The chief wants me to take him a large quake from the back of the house to cage a large, wonderful bird he caught at the farm," he told her.

"Make sure you take a strong one," she advised as she headed for the market.

Konehu made his way to the back of the house where he took the largest quake hanging from a pole. Situated nearby was the large storehouse of yams, corn, and sweet potatoes. Konehu wasted no time whatsoever. He made sure he filled the quake to the brim with the food items and, without letting anyone see him, slipped away quietly from that village.

Meanwhile, the chief waited patiently at his farm for over an hour, all the time pressing down on the palm leaves over the hole. And from time to time, he would look up to see if Konehu was returning. But Konehu was nowhere in sight. Anxious to have a closer look at the wonderful bird that was in the hole, he took a peek. To his surprise, the hole was just black and empty.

Surely, he must have been tricked. Then all of a sudden, it dawned on him that he was outwitted by no other than the much-talked-about Konehu.

Pounding rice in a mortar

~ 33 ~

How Tortoise Tricked Tiger

Tiger, one of the most fearsome animals in the jungle, feasted on the meat of deer and bush-hogs for his meals. But after a while, he got bored with the same type of meat over and over again, so he planned to kill the chief of the tortoises to satisfy his ravenous appetite.

Since he was not so sure about the strength of the slow-moving creature, he did not know how to go about getting him. He therefore worked out a plan whereby he pretended to be very friendly toward Tortoise in order to find out the power of his strength.

But Tortoise, being a very crafty animal, suspected that Tiger, who never spoke to him before, was up to some sort of mischief. So he knew he must be on guard all the time against this dangerous beast.

One morning, as Tortoise munched on some leaves by the riverside, Tiger quietly approached him.

"Hello, Tortoise," he called out. "What a nice day it is!"

"Good morning, Tiger," Tortoise replied.

"Well, I know you are very slow in your movement," observed Tiger. "So I wonder if you have enough strength to move over a long distance."

"Don't worry about that, my dear brother," retorted Tortoise. "I can move fast enough, and I'm stronger than you may even think."

"Well, you know that no one is stronger than I am," laughed Tiger. "I run very fast, I am a good hunter, I eat a lot of meat, and I am physically very strong."

"Anyone can boast of being strong," Tortoise responded. "I am strong as well. And who knows? Maybe I am stronger than you."

Tiger roared with laughter.

"You are a slow-moving creature with stumpy legs," he chuckled. "You can never be strong and fast as I am."

"Well, you have to prove that," said Tortoise.

"Then let us have a race," Tiger suggested. "I'm not sure if you are stronger, but at least I can prove I'm faster than you."

Tortoise considered this challenge for a moment.

"Agreed!" he said finally. "Tomorrow morning at this time, we will race along this track to the tall troolie palm yonder, then cross the river and continue along the track on the other side of the river, ending up at that tall *mora* tree just across from here."

"This will be such an easy victory for me," Tiger said. "We'll meet right here tomorrow morning for the race."

During the rest of that day, Tortoise visited three of his friends and told them of Tiger's big challenge. He cleverly worked out a plan with them and asked them to place themselves at different points along the race track the next morning.

So, the following day, Tiger met Tortoise as planned. They lined up at the starting point. Tiger called out, "Ready, steady, go!"

And away Tiger leaped, leaving Tortoise way behind.

But all this was part of Tortoise's plan. So he swam quickly over the narrow river and crawled under the big mora tree on the opposite bank to await Tiger's arrival.

Meanwhile, as Tiger galloped along, from time to time he would take a quick glance back to see how far behind Tortoise was. Then, just in front of him, he saw Tortoise crawling along the track. It was really Tortoise's friend, but how was he to know?

"This Tortoise can really move fast!" he mumbled.

So he decided that he must increase his speed. So like a fast-blowing wind, he flew past the slow-moving creature and laughed heartily. But then, as he neared the troolie palm near the river crossing, he spotted what looked like Tortoise crawling toward the water.

Tiger was truly amazed with this new development. "How did he get here so quickly?" he wondered as he sped by and leaped into the river. He swiftly swam across and began running toward the mora tree. As before, he looked back to see if Tortoise was close behind. About halfway between the crossing and the finishing line, he noticed Tortoise crawling ahead of him. Not knowing this was Tortoise's third friend, he panted, "How is he moving so quickly?"

With a great burst of speed, he raced past the slow animal and shouted, "Hah! Let me see how you can pass me now."

But to his amazement, when he was approaching the mora tree at the greatest speed, he saw Tortoise waiting there for him.

Tiger could hardly believe his eyes as he panted for breath.

"Well, well, well. You must admit I'm faster than you," Tortoise said.

"Yes, you've surely beaten me in this race," he admitted when he could finally breathe normally.

Then after he was well rested, he thought of another way he could prove his superiority over Tortoise.

"I think I am better at painting than you," he told Tortoise. "Let's have a painting contest. You paint my body, and I'll paint yours. This will test our skills to see who is more skillful."

Tortoise agreed to this new challenge, and after collecting a quantity of paint, they began the contest of painting each other's body. Tiger was sure that he was a better painter, but Tortoise, being slow and deliberate, mixed bright colors and applied them carefully on Tiger's body. But Tiger's painting was very poor, and he left rough marks and a drab gray paint on Tortoise's shell. On the other hand, when Tiger looked at himself, he saw his body decorated with colors ranging from bright brown, yellow, and shiny black. He was immensely pleased with his new appearance.

"Tortoise, I must admit you definitely have better painting skills," he said.

After admiring himself over and over again, Tiger told Tortoise, "You may be a faster runner and a better painter, but no one is better at hunting than I am."

"Don't be so sure of yourself," replied Tortoise.

"Well then, let's go into the forest and hunt a deer," suggested Tiger.

But Tortoise did not trust him since Tiger was very cunning.

"No, I will not go with you," he explained. "You go and chase the deer, and I will kill it."

So Tiger ran into the forest, saw a deer, and began to chase it along a pathway. Meanwhile, after Tiger departed, Tortoise found a tree with a broken, heavy, dead branch hanging over the pathway. He climbed up the tree and waited. As the deer ran under that same tree, Tortoise dropped the heavy branch on his neck, killing him instantly. Then he clambered down the tree, cut open the deer's carcass, smeared some of its blood on his own mouth, and awaited Tiger's arrival.

When Tiger appeared on the scene, he was shocked to see the dead deer and a bloody-mouthed Tortoise standing near to the carcass.

"I killed that deer you were chasing, and I have already eaten my share," he explained to Tiger.

Tiger was truly dumbfounded.

"I have to say, you're a very great hunter," he admitted.

From that day, Tiger no longer doubted Tortoise, and he no longer entertained the thought of having tortoise meat for his meal.

The tortoise

The trunk of a tall mora tree

~ 34 ~

How the Sun Was Set Free

A long, long time ago, the sun suddenly disappeared from the sky and thus could no longer light up the land and provide any warmth. The reason for this was that a selfish king in another land far to the east had imprisoned him in order to keep all the light and warmth for himself.

Meanwhile, in the west, Yuro, the farmer, lived on the bank of a great river with his wife and two beautiful teenage daughters. After learning of the sun's imprisonment, he decided to send his older daughter Maba to persuade the king to release the sun.

Maba set out on her long journey and had to walk for many days through the thick forest and cross wide rivers before she finally reached where the king lived.

Upon arriving at his home, she said to the king, "My father wants you to release the sun and put him back in the sky so he can shine his light for everyone."

The king pretended not to understand the girl's words and laughed at her.

"I haven't imprisoned the sun," he lied.

"I'm sure you have him locked up somewhere," Maba insisted. "Please release him so we can all have light in the land."

The king then looked at her affectionately and said, "I'll see what I can do, but first you have to agree to be my wife."

The girl felt that the king was extremely rude to her.

"Definitely not!" she responded. "I can never marry an insolent person like you."

Hearing the girl's response, the king became angry and rebuked her.

"You're a very stubborn girl," he shouted. "Leave my land immediately and don't ever return."

So Maba, unable to persuade the king to release the sun, made her way through the thick forest back to her home on the riverside.

As soon as she arrived home, she related everything to her father and about how the sun's captor had laughed at his request.

Undeterred by Maba's explanation, the father decided to send his second daughter, Saba—hoping that she would be better able to persuade the king.

On her way to the king's house, Saba crossed the thick jungle and rivers, but she took less time than her sister.

Approaching the king, she said, "My sister came before me, requesting that you release the sun from where you're keeping him and to put him in the sky so he can shine his light on everybody. I am here to make that same request."

But again he insisted, "I haven't imprisoned the sun."

"Then why is the place so dark? I'm sure you have him imprisoned nearby," the girl responded. "Please release him so he can light up the land."

This time, the king made the same proposal to her sister, "I'll see what I can do to help you find the sun, but you have to agree to be my wife."

"Certainly not!" she answered very quickly. "I cannot marry someone who is a liar."

The king immediately flew into a temper and shouted, "Get off my land, and don't ever come back!"

Angrily Saba shouted back at him, "You are an insolent person. You have no right to speak to me like that. I am going nowhere until you release the sun."

As she spoke, she kept looking around to see if she could find the place where the sun was hidden. In a far corner, she saw a very large bag tied to a wooden post and immediately suspected that was the hiding place.

The king, noticing that the girl was staring at the bulky bag, said quickly, "Careful! Don't even think about touching that bag!"

But the tone of his voice betrayed him, and the girl knew instantly that the sun was hidden in that bag. Ignoring his threats, she dashed toward the bag and ripped it open.

The bright, dazzling face of the sun was exposed immediately, and rays of light and heat quickly spread across the hills and forests and all over the land.

Knowing that his secret had been uncovered and he could no longer contain the power of the sun again, the king pushed him toward the east and then hung the ripped bag in the western sky, where it was lit up by the rays of the sun. This ripped bag then became the moon.

Meanwhile, Saba hurried away and finally reached her own home on the riverside where she described to her family how she had managed to free the sun from his hiding place.

Her father was very happy, and he and the other people enjoyed the beauty of the sun as it moved across the sky. But in a short while, they were disappointed as he disappeared behind the hills, leaving the rivers lit only by the reflection of the moon.

Naturally, Yuro felt dissatisfied that the sun spent such a short time in the sky. So he told Saba, "Go again to the east and wait for the sun to start his trip over the clouds. As soon as he begins to climb upward, carefully tie a tortoise on his tail. This will make him travel slowly."

Sometime after, Saba arrived at the place where the sun rested, and just before he began his journey into the sky, she quietly hooked a heavy tortoise to his tail. This added weight slowed him down considerably.

Ever since that day that Saba tied the tortoise to the sun's tail, the earth began to receive much longer periods of light during the day. The sun hides away at night, disappearing little by little into the waters of the sea. There he sleeps and refreshes himself by drinking lots and lots of water because, if he did not, he would die of the heat given off by his own rays.

Meanwhile, the moon quietly follows the sun's path, reflecting his light as he sinks far away in the west.

A river in Guyana's interior

~ 35 ~

The Precious Necklace

Juya, the great hunter who controlled the rain, had two wives, both of whom had magical powers. They were Mima who lived on the land deep in the great forest and Pulowi who dwelled at the bottom of the wide ocean.

Mima was very poor, but she survived by hunting deer and other small animals in her environment. On the other hand, Pulowi was very rich; and she controlled large groups of turtles, fish, and other sea animals. But above all, she possessed large quantities of expensive jewels made from various kinds of precious stones. Among the jewels more dear to her was a necklace of gold beads and red, white, and pink coral that she kept in a small silk sack. This small sack was then placed in a larger bag with her other jewels. And as a security measure, this large bag was then tied high up on the rafters over her bed.

All along, Mima had been very jealous of Pulowi's wealth, so she wondered how she could steal some of it. One day she called her friend, Juna the hummingbird, and confided in him her desire for Pulowi's jewels.

"Pulowi has everything," she told him. "I wish I can get my hands on her precious necklace."

"Well, I can steal it for you," the hummingbird suggested.

"But how can you get to the bottom of the sea?" asked Mimi. "Only those with magical powers can go there."

Upon hearing those words, the hummingbird chuckled. "Don't you know that I have magical powers?" he replied. "I can easily travel to Pulowi's home at the bottom of the sea."

Mima was rather thrilled to hear this. Excitedly she squealed, "Go, my friend, and bring Pulowi's necklace to me."

Away Juna flew with great speed over the deep forest until he reached the seashore.

There, using his magic powers, he changed himself into a young man and dived swiftly into the deep sea. Shortly after, he arrived at Pulowi's large house where she lived with her three daughters.

As Juna made his way up to Pulowi's front door, she looked at the strange young man in surprise.

"Young man, from where have you come?" she questioned. "I've never seen you around here before."

"My name is Juna. I've come from a place far away, and I'm traveling all over the world," he responded. "I've heard about you and your beautiful big house, so I have decided to come here to meet with you."

The young man's pleasant demeanor and refined manners captivated Pulowi, and she welcomed him warmly. After offering him refreshments, she said, "If you wish, you can stay with us for a few days."

Then she instructed her daughters, "Hang a hammock for Juna so he can get a comfortable place to sleep."

So Juna stayed at Pulowi's home and endeared himself to everyone—including Pulowi's servants—with his good manners, his cheerful way, and his willingness to assist with household chores. Very soon, he earned the trust of everyone in the house.

But, of course, all this was part of Juna's plan. Before daybreak on the third day of his visit, when everyone was still fast asleep, he changed himself back into his hummingbird form and very quietly flew high up under the roof to the rafters where the precious bag of jewels was secured. He carefully opened the bag and found the small silk sack containing the precious necklace. After removing it, he sealed the large bag and set it back in place.

Then tightly grabbing hold of the silk sack, he quietly flew from the bottom of the sea to the shore. He rested for a little while before flying over the deep forest where he delivered the sack to Mima.

Meanwhile, at daybreak, Pulowi stared at the big bag of jewelry hanging from the rafters. All of a sudden, she felt an urge to play with her jewels since that was one of her pleasurable pastimes. So she summoned one of her servants to climb a long ladder and release the bag and place it on her bed. But the very moment she opened her bag, she noticed that the small sack containing her most precious necklace was gone.

She was shocked beyond belief. Who could have stolen her necklace? There was only one stranger in their midst, and he must be the thief!

With much haste, she rushed out to Juna's hammock. But he was nowhere in sight! And so was her most valuable necklace.

She screamed, "Help me! That stranger stole my beautiful necklace."

Hearing her loud cries, her daughters and servants rushed to help her.

"How do you know he stole it?" her eldest daughter questioned.

"Well, he is not here anymore, and the silk sack with the necklace is gone." Pulowi cried and began to weep loudly. "What am I going to do?"

"Well, the thief is far gone," her second daughter moaned resignedly. "And that's a good lesson, to never trust a stranger no matter how pleasant he is."

But Pulowi was not yet ready to give up. She and her servants combed the entire sea for many days looking for Juna, but they never dreamed that he had changed into a hummingbird and had long returned to the land.

In the meantime, in the forest, Mima caressed the beautiful necklace, which she placed around her neck, for now she felt rich and extremely happy.

"Thank you, Juna, for bringing this beautiful necklace to me," she said.

"That's what friends are for," replied the hummingbird.

So as a reward, she presented the hummingbird with the silk sack in which the necklace was kept. "Take this silk sack and make yourself a new hammock," she told him.

To this day, the hummingbird still lives in a tiny nest that looks like a little silk sack.

And as for Pulowi, every time she thinks of her lost necklace, she flies into an awful rage with white foam running from her mouth. It is said that every time this happens, it causes terrible storms with foamy waves wreaking havoc on the seashore.

The hummingbird

~ 36 ~

The Lazy Man

Bunda was a lazy man who avoided, as much as possible, doing any strenuous work. One morning, he and the men of his riverside village went to the seaside in a large canoe to catch crabs. Meanwhile, their wives remained at home and made the paiwarri, which would be ready for their return in the evening.

The seaside was some distance away, and since paddling the canoe was a tiresome task, the men stopped at various intervals to rest on the riverbank.

At one of the resting places was a small kookrit palm with a large bunch of ripe fruit. They cut the bunch of kookrit and, placing it in the canoe, they continued on their journey. As they paddled, they plucked the ripe kookrit, peeled off the brown skin with their teeth, and ate the tasty yellowish meat covering the seed.

Meanwhile, Bunda, who did not relish the task of paddling, ate more than his fair share of the kookrit on the bunch. And as soon as he was finished eating the meaty parts, he threw the seeds into his quake.

Then he called out to his companions, "My friends, don't throw the seeds overboard. Throw them in my quake."

"Why are you collecting the kookrit seeds?" one of them asked.

"Oh, I'm collecting them for my children to play with," he responded.

So the men, after enjoying the tasty kookrit flesh, threw the seeds into Bunda's quake—which soon filled up.

It was not until midafternoon that they arrived at the seaside, and soon after, they began their hunt for crabs. But the lazy Bunda did not join them. Instead, he remained in the moored canoe, hoping that each of the men would give him a few crabs at the end of their hunt. But this was not to be.

After the crab hunt, with their quakes all filled to the brim, the men climbed into the canoe and set off for their home.

When they arrived at the village, it was already dark. So they left all their crab-filled quakes on the riverbank and walked to their respective homes. Bunda, with no shame whatsoever, left his quake of kookrit seeds in the collection as well.

Early the following morning, the men went with their wives to the riverbank to uplift their quakes so that they could prepare the crabs for cooking.

"Where is your quake?" Bunda's wife inquired.

"Oh, it is at the bottom of the pile," he quickly replied. "We have to wait until the others remove their quakes."

Indeed, his quake was at the bottom of the pile, and his wife picked it up and took it home.

Bunda's mother-in-law was also living at his house with his family. So she decided to help her daughter with the quakeful of crabs. They took it into the kitchen and opened it to see how many crabs it contained.

"My goodness!" Bunda's wife exclaimed. "The quake has only kookrit seeds."

Her mother peered into the quake.

"Well, you see what a lazy good-for-nothing you have as your husband," she grumbled. "All the other men brought home crabs, but Bunda brought home kookrit seeds."

"What shall we do with these all these seeds?" Bunda's wife wondered.

Her mother thought for a while.

"Oh yes, I know what you should do," she finally said. "Put all the seeds in a big pot and boil them until the hard shells crack open."

The wife, thereupon, put all the kookrit seeds into a big pot and set them to boil.

By this time, the other wives had heard from their husbands how Bunda refused to catch crabs and had only collected kookrit seeds in his quake. They were not too surprised since they knew of Bunda's laziness, so they each gave a quantity of crabs to his wife without his knowing about it. They also made sure she promised not to give Bunda any of the cooked crabs.

Later that same day, the family sat down to have their meal. Bunda's mother-in-law shared out cooked crabs to the children and to her daughter and poured out bowls of paiwarri for them to drink.

But in Bunda's bowl, she loaded boiled kookrit seeds.

Bunda observed his family eating cooked crabs heartily. Pointing to his bowl of hard kookrit seeds, he asked, "What is this?"

"Oh, those are the crabs you caught yesterday," his mother-in-law replied as she glared at him.

And so Bunda remained hungry since his wife and mother-in-law refused to share their crabs with him.

The next time the men went crab hunting, Bunda ensured he did his part of the job so he could take home his quake full of crabs. He certainly learnt his lesson, which cured him of his laziness.

Kookrit tree with bunches of fruit

Kookrit fruits

~ 37 ~

The Unlucky Man

Weyno, a young man, had two brothers-in-law who never seemed to like him. This was because each time he went out to hunt with them, he proved to be very unlucky. While they were able to kill deer, bush-hogs, and a variety of birds, Weyno's arrows always missed their targets; and he would return home in the evening empty-handed. As a result, his two brothers-in-law felt obliged, against their true wishes, to share their game with him.

And as time progressed, his brothers-in-law felt that he was much too unlucky as a hunter, so they secretly plotted to get rid of him.

One day, they all went into the forest on a hunting expedition. After covering a great distance along a narrow forest trail, they reached a point where the trail forked into two different directions.

"Look here, Weyno," his older brother-in-law said, "we will go along this side of the trail while you go along the other."

"Why can't we go together?" Weyno inquired with a puzzled look on his face.

"You see, Weyno, we stand a better chance to kill more animals if we split up," his brother-in-law explained. "There are deer and bush-hogs in both directions, so we would be better off to hunt both ways."

Even though he disliked the plan, he grudgingly agreed to go alone because, eventually, they would all meet later at the same trail junction.

But his two devious brothers-in-law deliberately sent him along that particular trail since it led to the area where the ferocious *Black Tiger* lived. They hoped that this huge beast would devour him.

The poor, innocent Weyno knew nothing that he was being sent willfully into Black Tiger's territory, so armed with his sharp cutlass and bow and arrows, he cautiously walked along the trail, looking to spot deer and bush-hogs. But he saw none of these and continued walking until he arrived at a point where the trail unexpectedly became wider.

Then all of a sudden, a loud rushing noise shattered the silence of the forest. With much alarm, he exclaimed, "What is that?"

And right then he knew exactly what it was, for he came face to face with the big, ferocious Black Tiger. The beast rushed at him from behind the bushes, but in a flash, Weyno dashed in the opposite direction toward a huge mora tree. With great speed, Black Tiger raced after him.

Luckily, Weyno managed to get quickly to the tree and ran round and round the trunk with Black Tiger roaring behind him.

As they sped around the tree trunk, Weyno found himself close to Black Tiger's tail; and with a swift slash with his cutlass, he cut off the beast's back legs. Immediately, the tiger was immobilized. As the beast tumbled to the ground in great pain, Weyno shot an arrow in his neck, killing him instantly.

After resting for a while, he returned to the trail junction, but he saw none of his brothers-in-law. So he waited there for them until darkness crept in, but after they failed to show up, he decided to return home.

By this time, his wicked brothers-in-law were absolutely sure that Black Tiger had finished him off. So when they returned home, they pretended to be very worried.

"Where is Weyno?" their sister (Weyno's wife) asked.

"We don't know," the second brother replied. "He left to hunt along a separate trail, and after he did not return to our meeting place, we decided to come home."

And at that very moment that they were conveying that untruth, Weyno stepped into the house.

Showing great surprise, his elder brother-in-law lied, "Where were you? We waited for you at the meeting place, but after we did not see you, we thought you came home by yourself."

And with all that, Weyno still did not suspect his brothers-in-law had planned to get rid of him.

"Why couldn't you wait a bit longer?" he wanted to know.

"Well, we thought you came home, but after we did not see you here, we were thinking that we would have to search for you," his younger brother-in-law explained.

By this time, Weyno could hide his excitement no longer.

"If only you had waited, you would have learnt that I killed Black Tiger today," he shouted in glee.

All the family members, who had gathered by this time, were astounded to hear such great news.

"You killed Black Tiger?" his elder brother-in-law sneered. "You can't even kill a bush-hog, and now you're telling us you killed the terrible Black Tiger when the best hunters have failed to do so."

"I myself can't believe this," Weyno's father-in-law said with much doubt. "I have to see the dead Black Tiger myself."

"All right, all right," Weyno assured his father-in-law and brothers-in-law. "Tomorrow morning, we will go to the spot where I killed him."

So, early the next morning, they all returned to the forest; and as they approached the huge mora tree, they saw Black Tiger lying on the ground.

"Are you sure he is dead?" the old man asked.

"I'm absolutely sure," Weyno assured him. "Apparently, you still do not believe me."

Leaving them standing a little distance away, Weyno walked up to the dead beast and placed his foot on his head.

"Don't be afraid," he called out to them. "Come and have a look."

Only then did Weyno's father-in-law and brothers-in-law muster the courage to approach the dead Black Tiger. And being satisfied that the beast was dead, they wended their way home in amazement that the unlucky Weyno could have been so brave to kill the dangerous Black Tiger.

By the end of the day, everyone learned of Weyno's courageous feat, and soon after, the people appointed him as the village chief.

But although he achieved such great honors from his villagers, yet he was not satisfied, for he knew he had poor luck in hunting animals.

So he decided to consult Wowta, the tree frog who was originally a witch. He searched in the forest for the tree in which she lived and called out, "Wowta! Wowta, I need your help."

But no answer came from Wowta.

"Wowta, I need your help," he continued calling out. "I want you to give me better luck when I'm hunting."

But despite all his persistent pleas, there still was no response. By that time, darkness crept over the land, so he decided to try another method to get Wowta's attention.

He started to weep deliberately, for he knew that anyone would pity a weeping person. And as he wailed under the tree, a large flock of birds of all sizes walked by very near to him. And as they did so, they each rubbed against him.

After the birds, up came a large group of forest animals including acouris, labbas, deer, bush-hogs, tapirs, tigers, and snakes; and they all took turns and rubbed lightly against him as well.

But Weyno was unaware that the actions of all those animals resulted from Wowta's magic, for she indeed felt pity for him as he wept. And as each animal or bird rubbed against Weyno, he became gifted with the power to hunt that particular creature. But, of course, Weyno knew nothing of this at that time.

It was not until daylight that all the forest creatures finished marching by near to Weyno.

Not long after, Weyno noticed a strange old woman approaching with an arrow in her hand. It was Wowta, who had changed from a tree frog into this woman.

"So you are the man whose loud crying kept me awake the entire night?" she asked.

"Yes," he replied.

"Well, I will help you get rid of your bad luck," she told him. "Look on your left arm from your shoulder down to your wrist."

Looking down, he saw that it was covered with a green fungus. He was very much confused.

"Scrape off that fungus," she instructed. "That is the fungus that brings bad luck."

So with a piece of stick, he quickly scraped the green fungus off his arm. Wowta then took Weyno's old arrow and handed him the one she carried.

"Fix this arrow on your bow and shoot at that vine hanging on that tree over there," she ordered.

Weyno did as he was instructed and was astounded when the arrow went straight to its target.

"Now remove the arrow from the vine and shoot it into the air," she said.

He did so, and the arrow brought down a big powis.

"Remove the arrow, and shoot anywhere you desire," she told him.

Weyno fired the arrow, and every time he did so, it brought down a game animal or bird. He was elated. Soon, he had accumulated a few large birds, labbas, deer, and bush-hogs.

"Now you can see the magical qualities of the arrow," Wowta said. "You may keep it, but never tell anyone how you got it."

"I will keep this secret," he solemnly promised as Wowta walked into the bushes and disappeared from sight.

After butchering the game, Weyno hurried home to his wife and in-laws who watched in astonishment as he displayed the large quantity of meat on a table.

"You are indeed a great hunter now," admitted his father-in-law.

Since that day, on every hunting trip, Weyno would always return home with great success.

This change in luck caused everyone to wonder how he managed to improve his hunting prowess. When asked, he refused to reveal the secret, but people persistently pressed him for an answer.

And of all the people, his brothers-in-law were more persistent than ever. One day they invited him to a grand feast of paiwarri, which he loved very much. And as he drank, he became more and more intoxicated. Then he began to talk freely, and it was then that he revealed the entire secret of his special magical arrow.

By the next morning when he was sober again, he decided to go out hunting. As he reached for his magical arrow he instead found his old arrow that Wowta had earlier taken from him. And ever since that day, his bad luck returned, and he earnestly wished that he had not broken that promise he made to Wowta.

The black puma (Guyana's "black tiger")

The labba

~ 38 ~

Bat Mountain

A long time ago, a huge bat lived in one of the caves in the Kanuku mountain range. This huge monster created terror in the lowland savannah villages where the Makushi people lived. For, as soon as darkness stepped in, it flew out of its cave down to the villages and grabbed, in its sharp powerful claws, any villager who happened to be outside of his hut. Then he flew away with his screaming prey to his home high up the mountainside where he tore him apart and feasted on the bloody flesh.

For this very reason, fear stalked the land, so everyone tried to be indoors before darkness fell. Despite such precaution, almost every morning, the various villages reported that one, two, or even three persons were found missing. Terrified screams at night and bloodstains seen on the ground in the morning were vivid evidence that the monster bat had done its bloody deed.

In an effort to escape this monster, some people abandoned their villages and moved to safer areas deep within the forest. But the giant bat, nevertheless, continued its deadly hunt at night. The population of the villages declined rapidly with the continued killings and the steady migration, and there was a feeling that the villages would become totally uninhabited.

From time to time, groups of men armed with spears and bows and arrows climbed up the mountains in search of the bat's hideout, but they all failed in their search. Even the piamen of the villages used all their magic powers to prevent the attacks, but they, too, failed to stop the bat from abducting people at night.

Finally, a very old woman from one of the villages decided that she would stop the monster from continuing his deadly attacks. She revealed a plan of how she would kill this bat and save all the people in the villages. But the villagers, who had deep respect for her, pleaded, "No! No! We don't want you to put yourself in such a dangerous position."

But the old woman was adamant.

"Look here," she explained. "I am an old woman, and I don't have long to live. If someone does not stop this terrible beast, everyone will surely be killed."

With all their pleadings, the villagers could do nothing to make her change her mind, so they finally let her carry out her plan.

So one night, she sat alone on a wooden stool in the middle of the village as she held on to a piece of burning wood. The other villagers remained in their homes in fear and peered through their windows at the old woman as she waited for the huge bat to arrive.

Soon came the flapping of heavy wings, and the bat swiftly swooped down on her in the dark village square. He grabbed her with its heavy claws and flew away to its hidden cave on the mountainside. She suffered agonizing pains as the bat dropped her on the cave floor and tore away at her flesh. But she managed to throw the burning firewood at the mouth of the cave where it began to burn the dry grass in the locality. Far below, the villagers spotted the flames and knew immediately that was where the bat's cave would be found.

The next morning, a large band of men, fully armed, climbed the mountain to the area where the fire burned. In a very short time, they found the hidden cave with the huge monster bat sleeping soundly inside. Quickly, they shot and killed the monster with their sharp poison-arrows. Then the villagers conducted a search for the old woman but discovered only a huge heap of dried bones. Certainly, these were the bones of the bat's victims, including those of the poor old woman who sacrificed herself to save the villages.

The Kanuku Mountains

~ 39 ~

The Legend of the Victoria Regia

Many years ago, there was a little forest village on the bank of a wide river in southern Guyana. All of the inhabitants were very happy as they always reaped good crops from their gardens, and wild animals they hunted for meat were abundant in the forests on both sides of the river.

In this forest village lived twelve teenage girls who always gathered in the evenings under a tall mora tree on the riverside to sing songs their mothers had taught them. After their singing, as the moon rose from beneath the horizon and the stars twinkled in the dark sky, the girls would stare in awe at these beautiful heavenly bodies.

They became particularly interested in these attractive objects since there was a general belief in those days of long ago that anyone who touched anything beautiful would acquire some of its beauty.

"The moon and the stars are so lovely," said Neca, one of the girls in the group. "I wish we could touch them so we can acquire some of their beauty, but they are so far away."

"We must find a way to touch them," replied another girl in the group. "Maybe, we should climb to the top of the mountain, and from there we will be able to do so."

Every evening after their singing session, they stared at the moon and the stars and contemplated various ways they could attempt to touch them.

Of all the girls, Neca was more interested in touching the moon, and in the evening she spent long hours just staring at it as it moved slowly across the night sky.

"I know what I will do," she declared to her friends one evening. "I will climb to the top of this tall mora tree and try to touch the moon."

"Well, you may climb to the top of the tree, but I think we can touch the moon and the stars if we go to the top of the mountain," one of her friends explained. This view seemed to be more popular, and all, except Neca, decided that they would do exactly that.

One night when the full moon was rising in the sky, Neca climbed to the top of the mora tree and stretched out her hands toward the shining orb. But, clearly, the moon was too far away for her to accomplish this feat. In great disappointment, she descended and tearfully went home to sleep.

Meanwhile, that same night her friends walked through the forest to the high mountain some distance away from the village. After reaching the peak, they stretched out their hands toward the moon and the stars, but they, too, failed to attain their objective. With long, sad faces, they wearily walked back home now fully aware that they could never acquire the beauty of those distant objects.

But Neca never gave up. The following night, when her friends had all gone to sleep, she walked along the riverbank once again and stared at the big golden moon as it rose above the trees. Then she looked into the calm water of the river and there she observed the moon's glowing reflection.

"Now, this is how I can touch the moon," she reasoned. And with that, she plunged into the river and reached out to the reflection. But she soon disappeared beneath the deep still water and was never seen again.

But the moon goddess did see Neca as she made that fateful plunge.

"I truly pity her," she sighed. "Neca always wanted to become more beautiful than ever, so I'll ensure that people will admire that beauty for all times."

So the moon goddess, from the depths of the river, brought up Neca's body—which she transformed into a large majestic pink water lily in the water near the riverbank. From that day, people everywhere became fascinated with this most gorgeous flower growing beside its large circular lily pad.

Today, that stately and attractive water lily is widely known as the Victoria Regia.

The Victoria Regia lily

~ 40 ~

The Fisherman and the Water Goddess

Manoo, a young fisherman, resided in a little village on the riverbank. He was held in high esteem by the other villagers because he invariably caught a large amount of fish on a regular basis. His old mother, who lived with him, was very proud of his skills, and she helped to clean and smoke-dry some of the catch from time to time.

One day, Manoo set out downriver in his canoe to an area rich with large fishes. He threw out his fishing line, and shortly after, he felt a bite on his bait. He quickly drew in his line, but caught nothing. He threw out his line four more times, but even though he felt sharp tugs at the bait, he failed to make a single catch.

After resting for a while, he continued to throw his fishing line but again failed every time to catch any fish on that day. As a result, he became disheartened with the failure of this fishing trip, so he finally decided to return home.

"Let me make a final throw before I go," he mumbled.

With that, he rebaited the hook and threw out the line for the final time.

Suddenly, he felt a sharp pull on the line.

So, with much excitement, he shouted, "Good! I've caught a big one now!"

Though heavy, he hauled in the line rapidly, and to his amazement, he saw that the hook was entangled in the long hair of a beautiful young woman whom he pulled safely into his canoe.

After he recovered from this shock, he managed to untangle the fishing hook from her hair.

"Who are you?" he inquired, still astounded at what had just happened.

And the young woman replied, "I am Oriyu, the water goddess."

Manoo had heard of the water goddess before, but he never thought that she lived in this river.

"You are indeed a beautiful young woman," he declared. "But why do you tangle yourself on my fishing line?"

She replied, "I've watched you every time you fished on this river, and knowing of your good reputation, I believe my fate is to live on the land with you."

"It will be my honor to have you as my wife," he said with much excitement.

"Before I can be your wife, you have to make one promise," she responded.

"And what must I promise?" he asked.

"Well, you must introduce me to your mother, but neither she nor you must ever tell anyone who I am," she explained.

"I promise you faithfully, I will never tell anyone this secret. And I'm sure my mother will do the same," he told her.

Late that evening, Manoo took her home to meet his mother, who was happy to see her son in the company of a beautiful young woman. After he explained who Oriyu was, he implored his mother not to divulge this information to anyone.

"My dear Oriyu, I will never let anybody know that you are the water goddess," she promised faithfully.

So Manoo took Oriyu as his wife, and she became his faithful companion on all his fishing trips. And since she had the ability to see clearly way down to the depths of the riverbed, she advised him where large groups of fish were located and would tell him when to throw out his fishing line. Soon, they would catch a sizeable quantity of fish, which they would take back home.

Manoo's mother was excited to see this steady supply of fish, some of which she bartered with her neighbors for other food supplies, such as vegetables and meat, and cotton fabrics to make clothing.

One afternoon, as the old woman and her friends were having fun at a neighbor's house and drinking paiwarri, they all became intoxicated and laughed uproariously at their jokes and chatted noisily.

Then one of her friends asked her, "How do your son and daughter-in-law manage to catch more fish than anyone else in this neighborhood?"

And the old woman, her tongue now loose with the quantity of paiwarri she had consumed, replied, "Well, it's because my daughter-in-law has magic powers, and she can see where the fishes are swimming in the river."

Upon hearing this, all the others suddenly became silent and tuned in on the conversation.

"How does she have these magic powers?" the neighbor inquired.

Forgetting her promise, the old woman answered excitedly, "Because my daughter-in-law is Oriyu, the water goddess!"

The others were stunned at this revelation.

"No wonder she is such a beautiful young woman," one of them commented. "And she certainly knows where all the fishes are to be found in the rivers."

Suddenly, the old woman knew she had spoken too much and that she had revealed the secret of Oriyu's origin. She quietly put down her paiwarri cup and, in great remorse, departed for her home.

Late that afternoon, Manoo and Oriyu returned to the village with a large quantity of fish. As they walked on the path to their home, other villagers gathered around and stared excitedly at Oriyu.

"Dear goddess, we are so happy to have you living among us," they said.

Oriyu all at once knew that her mother-in-law had exposed her secret, but when she arrived home, she did not express any anger whatsoever toward the old woman. But now that her secret was revealed, she was aware that she could no longer live on the land with her husband.

About a month later, the season arrived when very large groups of crabs from the ocean marched to the shore. People from all the villages set out in their canoes for the seashore to gather these marching crabs and store them in quakes. Cooked crab was a delicacy, and everyone looked forward to gather as much as possible.

Oriyu and Manoo also set out on this expedition, but when their canoe was in the middle of the river, she shouted to the others, "My husband and I are going to visit my relatives below the water. We will not be long, but we will send up food and drink, which you must share fairly."

Then she held Manoo's arm, and they both dived into the river. Shortly after, a large wooden jar floated to the surface and was quickly pulled on board one of the canoes. In the jug was a large bottle of casiri and a quantity of sweet potatoes, all of which the villagers consumed. They then threw the empty jug and the potato skins back into the river. Immediately, Oriyu's magic changed the jug into the giant river fish, the *lau-lau,* and the potato skins into tiny fish known as *imiri.*

As for Oriyu and Manoo, they never returned to the land. But the older people still remember the events of that day when they departed. And up to this day, they say the lau-lau is the fisherman's water jug, and the little imiri is his sweet potato.

Newer houses in an Amerindian village

Traditional Amerindian houses

~ 41 ~

The Pot Under the Benab

Pedro lived with his wife and two sons in a little village near the forest. One day, as he hunted for bush-hogs, he came across a small benab built on a small clearing in the forest. And since he was very tired after following the trail of a pack of the wild pigs, he decided to rest there for a while. As he entered the shady *benab*, he was surprised to see a medium-sized iron pot with contents boiling on a small fireplace.

"Somebody must have left this pot boiling here," he murmured to himself.

But as soon as he uttered those words, he was shocked to hear a voice coming directly from the pot, "No one owns me, and I am an exceptional pot with special powers."

Pedro could not believe what he was hearing.

Then the pot spoke once again, "Are you hungry?"

"Yes," Pedro replied without hesitation.

"What would you like to eat?" the pot asked.

"Well, I really like bird meat," Pedro answered, still very amazed.

"Tell me, 'I am hungry. Cook some bird meat for me'," the pot instructed.

So Pedro followed the pot's instruction and said, "I am hungry. Cook some bird meat for me."

The pot made some bubbling boiling sounds and instantly became filled with delicious cooked bird meat.

"Here is your meal," the pot said. "Eat as much as you want."

And seeing that Pedro was quite hungry, and being a glutton also, he quickly gobbled up all the meat in no time.

Leaving the marvelous pot still simmering on the fire, Pedro returned home quite satisfied. However, he kept this exciting discovery to himself, not even disclosing it to his own wife and sons.

That same evening, his wife prepared a lovely dinner of fish and offered it to him.

"No, no, I'm not hungry," he told her. "I will skip dinner this evening."

His wife was quite surprised since Pedro never refused food.

Two days later, Pedro returned to the forest and made his way to the benab. As before, the pot was steaming on the fire and he ordered it, "I am hungry. Cook some bush-hog meat for me."

The pot bubbled, and in a flash, it was full of steaming bush-hog meat. In great delight, Pedro stuffed himself with all the meat and did not even leave a little scrap behind. Patting his bulging belly, he told the pot, "I'll be back in two days' time."

On his return home, his wife offered him a meal of cassava for dinner, but as before, he refused to eat it.

"I ate a lot of forest fruits today," he gave as his excuse. "I'm not hungry at all."

And so, every two days, he returned to the forest benab and ordered the enchanted pot to cook a special meal for him. He gorged himself every time and, in the evening, refused to eat the dinner his wife prepared with the excuse that he was not hungry at all.

But after this trend continued for about two weeks, his sons became suspicious that their father was up to something.

"That is so strange," the older son said. "Every time Father goes to the forest, he always says he is not hungry."

"We should follow him and see what he does," his brother suggested. "I believe he is getting a lot of food some place in the forest."

As a result, they agreed to keep an eye on their father. Two days later, as he set out for the forest, they secretly followed him. Hidden in the bushes, they watched as he entered the benab and saw him approaching a steaming pot. Then, to their amazement, they heard their father telling the pot, "I am hungry. Cook some deer meat for me."

Wide-eyed, they watched as the pot bubbled and became suddenly full of cooked deer meat, and saw their greedy father stuffing himself with all the contents of the pot.

Not wanting to alert their father to their presence, they quietly slipped away and made their way back home.

"Well, we now know Father's secret," the younger brother stated.

"Yes," the other replied. "But he is very selfish to have all that food for himself and not sharing any with our family."

As usual, that evening, Pedro refused the dinner of boiled sweet potatoes his wife prepared, saying that he had eaten fruits in the forest.

The next morning, Pedro joined some of his neighbors to fish for *morocut* in a river some distance away from the village. The two boys seized that opportunity of their father's absence and rushed to the forest benab where the pot simmered on the fire.

Remembering what their father told the pot, the elder brother said, "I am hungry. Cook some deer meat for me."

With mouths agape, they watched as the pot bubbled and filled itself with cooked deer meat. Then the two sat down near the pot and helped themselves to the hearty meal.

They were about to leave the benab when the younger brother said, "We must not let Father know we used the pot."

"You are correct," his brother agreed. "We have to clean the pot to remove all the traces of the food we made it cook for us."

Accordingly, they took the pot to a nearby stream, scrubbed it clean, then placed it back over the fire and returned home.

The next morning, Pedro returned home with the *morocut* he had caught. His wife fried some of the fish and offered it to him.

"No, no," he said, "I'm not hungry right now."

All the time, he was planning to slip away into the forest benab to get a big delicious meal from the special pot. Soon after, he told his wife, "Two days ago, I set some bird traps in the forest. I will go to see if they caught any."

With that excuse, he hurried away to the forest benab. The pot was still on the fire, and he ordered it, "I am hungry. Cook some pepperpot for me."

But the pot failed to respond to his command.

He shouted at it, "I am hungry. Cook some pepperpot for me."

Again, there was no response from the pot, for it had lost its magical powers when the two boys scrubbed it clean the day before.

Pedro was indeed now very hungry, and he wept in disappointment, fully aware that the pot had lost its magical powers and would no longer cook meals for him again.

A benab on the savannah

~ 42 ~

How Yawarri Starved Himself to Death

A lengthy drought hit the entire country, and it resulted in a widespread scarcity of food. As a result, all the animals moved across the savannah and into the forest to collect what little food they could find there.

One day, Yawarri, the big "bush-rat," came across old gray Tortoise plodding slowly through the dry savannah grass.

"Good day, Tortoise," Yawarri greeted him. "How are these hard times treating you?"

"Good day to you too, Yawarri," Tortoise replied. "It is really tough finding something to eat these days."

"I agree totally," responded Yawarri. "But how do you manage to survive in these days when it is so difficult to find anything to eat?"

"I manage quite well through my own wisdom," Tortoise said. "You see, I have experienced this problem of drought and food shortage many times before."

"So how do you manage?" asked Yawarri, now very eager to know.

"Well, what I do is to go without food for a few days at a time," explained Tortoise. "I can fast for long periods—longer than anybody else."

Now Yawarri was very vain, and he did not like to hear that anyone was his better. He never fasted a day in his life, but he did not want old Tortoise to feel superior to him.

"Oh, I fast as well, and I survive quite well too," he lied.

Tortoise looked at him and sneered, "You, Yawarri? You can't do without food at all, and I don't believe you can fast for even one day."

Yawarri felt insulted, and he shouted back, "I bet you I can fast longer than you."

"All right, all right," Tortoise laughed. "You don't have to get angry. I will accept your bet and show you I can fast longer than you."

So they set about discussing plans how to prove who was better at going without food. Finally, they decided that each would take a turn to choose a tree under which the other would be fenced in and would not eat any food until the tree began to produce ripe fruit.

Accordingly, Yawarri found a plum tree, built a strong fence around it, and locked up Tortoise inside. Every day, Yawarri visited Tortoise and shouted as he leaned against the fence, "Are you still alive?"

And Tortoise, sitting under the tree with his head tucked in his shell, shouted back, "Yes, I am alive. I can fast for a long time."

Day after day, and week after week, Yawarri came to the plum tree to check on Tortoise who showed no sign he was ever becoming weak with the long period of fasting.

After five months had elapsed, the plum tree produced flowers, and within another month, it was full of ripe fruits. So Yawarri broke down the fence and set Tortoise free.

"Well, you certainly proved you could fast for a long time," he told him. "But you will see I will do even better."

It was now Tortoise's turn to find a tree for Yawarri's test. He finally located a wild cashew tree, around which he also erected a strong fence and locked away his rival inside. Day after day, he visited as well and shouted over the fence, "Are you still alive, Yawarri?"

And Yawarri always answered, "Yes, I am fully alive!"

After two weeks had passed, Tortoise asked the regular question, "Are you alive, Yawarri?"

But this time, Yawarri responded somewhat weakly, "Yes, I am alive, but I am a bit tired."

"Don't you want to eat some food and give up the bet?" inquired Tortoise.

"Never!" responded Yawarri. "I'll show you I can fast longer than you."

Despite his severe hunger, he was still as vain as ever and would not admit to Tortoise that he wanted the bet to be called off.

After a month had elapsed, he could hardly move, and when Tortoise came near to the fence and asked if he was still alive, he barely croaked, "Yes, I am alive, but very tired."

When six weeks were completed, Tortoise returned to the enclosure and shouted, "Yawarri, are you alive?"

This time, there was no answer.

Tortoise peered through a small hole in the fence and saw that Yawarri was no longer alive. His body was stretched out under the tree, and it was already covered with flies. All along, Tortoise knew that Yawarri could never fast for long and, in any case, would not have survived if he had to wait for the wild cashew tree to bear fruit. Actually, Tortoise had purposely selected that particular tree since he was sure that Yawarri did not know that it produced fruit only once every three years.

And so it was because of vanity and his stubbornness that Yawarri gave up his own precious life just because of a simple bet.

The yawarri

~ 43 ~

The Stolen Girl

In a little village on the forest's edge lived a young couple and their one-year-old daughter. One early morning, the husband went into the forest to hunt while his wife remained at home to do the household chores. Later in the afternoon, she began preparing dinner as she waited for her husband to return home. While she was busy with this activity, the baby began to cry, so her attention was divided between her meal preparation and intermittent attempts to soothe the child.

As she was rocking the crying baby in her arms, an old woman appeared at her door.

"Let me help you with the baby," she volunteered.

During those times, it was not unusual for women in the village to assist each other with domestic chores and child care, so the wife happily accepted the much-needed assistance.

"Thanks for helping," she said and handed the baby over to the old woman.

"I'll take the baby to my home so you can finish your cooking in peace," the old woman told her.

And so the woman took the baby, who was now no longer crying, to her home at the far end of the village.

As soon as the wife had completed preparation of the meal, she walked over to the old woman's house.

"I've come to take my baby home," she told her.

But to her surprise, the old woman said, "What baby are you talking about?"

"You took my baby a while ago while I was preparing dinner," she reminded the old woman.

"You must be mistaken," the old woman retorted. "I never took your baby from you. You can come into my house and see for yourself that there is no baby here."

Without any hesitation, the young woman quickly ran into the house and looked all around, but she did not see her baby. In desperation, she began to weep loudly and then ran to her home to await her husband's arrival from his hunting trip.

Unknown to the young wife, this old woman was really Tiger in disguise since he had magical powers and could change himself into any form. He wanted the baby girl for himself, and for that reason, he presented himself to the young woman as a motherly old woman. And soon after taking the baby girl, he had hidden her away in his forest home.

In the meantime, the husband had returned home, and his wife—with tears streaming down her grief-stricken face—related the disastrous event to him. The two of them returned to the old woman's home but, to their great surprise, discovered that she was no longer there. Little did they know that the old woman had changed back into Tiger, her real self, and disappeared into the forest.

Overcome with much grief, the couple alerted the other villagers of their daughter's disappearance. Everyone made a diligent search all over the village and its surroundings, but without any success. The next morning, the search continued, but to no avail.

In great distress, the parents continued their search, but after a week, they gave up their quest. As time went by, they knew their baby daughter was lost forever, and that pain of losing her gradually faded as the years went by.

After sixteen years had passed, the couple noticed that certain small items were disappearing from their house. Beads and necklaces mysteriously vanished. Belts, aprons, and even small pots in the kitchen suddenly could not be found. They continued to lose other items, but they had no clue whatsoever as to why or how they were removed from the house.

However, they did not know that it was Tiger who was quietly stealing all the items for the girl to use. She had, by this time, matured into a beautiful young maiden as she continued to live in Tiger's forest home.

In the meantime, Tiger cared for her as his own daughter and provided all the clothes, food, and nourishment she needed at this age. By this time, the girl became fully aware of their physical differences, so one day, she questioned him about this.

"We are completely different," she stated. "Why is it that I am living with you and not with those who look like me?"

By now, Tiger felt the time had come for her to know more about herself.

"You are a human being, and I took you from your mother when you were just a baby," Tiger explained. "But you are now my daughter, and I will not send you away."

But the girl wanted to know more about herself and, from time to time, questioned Tiger.

One time she asked him, "Where do my real parents live?"

Tiger sensed that by asking him questions about her parents, she had intentions to escape from him. Despite this, he told her, "Your parents live in a house in the village near to this forest. I often went there secretly to bring away beads, aprons, and other things you needed."

"When will I get to meet my parents?" she asked with much anxiety.

"I will never allow you to leave as long as I am alive," Tiger angrily stated.

"Well, at least you can describe my parents' house," the girl said.

Tiger described the house in great detail, even though he was now more suspicious that the girl wanted to escape, and so he kept a close eye on her.

One evening she told him, "You are getting old, and I want to know what will happen to me when you die."

Again in anger, he shouted at her, "I have a long time to live, and you will remain here with me."

By this time, she had become determined to escape, so she waited for the right opportunity. Indeed, she was tired of being alone in the forest, and she wanted to be with other human beings like herself.

Finally, one day, she decided to make the final break. She placed a big pot on the fire and commenced preparing a huge meal. When the contents were boiling hot, she attempted to remove the pot from the fire. Pretending that the heat was too much for her to bear, she turned to Tiger.

"The pot is too heavy," she explained. "Please help me remove it from the fire."

Without any delay, Tiger stooped down, put his paws one on each side of the projecting rim of the pot, and lifted it off the fire. But while he was doing this, the girl hit the bottom of the pot and all the boiling contents splashed on the beast's face. He roared in severe pain, fell to the floor, and shortly after, he was dead.

Without any delay, the girl hurried away from Tiger's home and ran until she came out of the forest. She spotted the village in the distance and soon recognized her parents' home as was described earlier by Tiger.

She ran up to the house and shouted, "I am the girl that was lost a long, long time ago. Where are my parents?"

As she uttered those words, the parents rushed from the house and saw the girl standing outside.

"You are indeed our long lost daughter," the mother cried. "We are so happy to have you back with us."

Later, as she sat in her parents' home, she explained how Tiger had stolen her in the first place and she described in every little detail how she finally managed to escape from her captor. The parents sat and listened with great interest and were overjoyed to finally have their only daughter back where she belonged.

Amerindian handicraft items

~ 44 ~

Adaba, the Magic Frog

A family of three bothers and their eighteen-year-old sister, Simi, lived in the village near the forest. One day, they decided to hunt for bush-hogs and deer. The brothers decided to set up a camp site in the forest by erecting a benab under which they slung their hammocks, and then left Simi to prepare a meal while they departed to hunt for game. However, they were not very lucky that day, and when they returned to the benab late in the afternoon, all they managed to bring back were a few powis.

The next day, the brothers continued to hunt, but again they only managed to shoot six more powis with their arrows. Over the next two days they still continued to hunt hoping that they would get lucky and shoot some bush-hogs or a deer. But they could not get close to these animals and had to be content with shooting some more powis which fed in the tall bushes.

Each day as the brothers hunted, Simi remained at the benab and prepared the meal for them. After cooking, she had nothing else to do except to listen to the whistles and screeches of the birds on the tree-tops.

Not far from the benab was a large hollow tree. One morning, after her brothers had departed, she heard a loud croaking coming from within the hollow space of that tree. Wondering what it could be, she peeped through a hole in the trunk and saw a frog with striped legs sitting in a small pool of water in the hollow space.

"Why are you making all that noise?" she asked. "You should stop all that noise and bring me some meat to eat."

To her surprise, the frog immediately became silent, jumped out from the hollow tree, and changed himself into a young man armed with bow and a handful of arrows. Simi was thunderstruck with fear.

"Who are you?" the frightened girl asked in amazement.

"Don't be afraid," the young man replied trying to calm her. "I am Adaba, and as a frog I have magic powers to change myself into human form."

After a brief conversation, Adaba rushed away into the bushes and about two hours later returned with a quantity of bush-hog meat.

"You wanted meat to eat," he said. "Cook this before your brothers come back, for, as before, they will bring only powis."

And indeed, just as Adaba predicted, the brothers returned late that afternoon with some more powis. They were indeed very amazed to see their sister barbecuing a large quantity of meat while a strange young man relaxed in a hammock. And the young man was strange indeed because he had stripes running down his thin legs and he was dressed only in a loin cloth.

"Who are you?" the eldest brother inquired.

"My name is Adaba," he answered. "I met your sister here and she asked me to get some meat for her. I shot a bush-hog and that is the meat she is barbecuing."

Meanwhile, Simi kept her little secret, not revealing to her brothers that Adaba was really a frog transformed into a man.

"But how did you find a bush-hog when we could not shoot any for the past few days?" the second brother asked.

"I believe your arrows are not too good," Adaba replied. "Let me see what they look like."

When they showed him their arrows, he roared with laughter.

"These arrows can never shoot big animals," he chuckled. "See how much fungus is growing on them? You have to remove that stuff or else the arrows will never hit their targets."

Having explained this little technical detail, Adaba assisted the brothers in cleaning their arrows and decided to teach them the skills of shooting. He then asked them to stretch a fishing line between two trees a little distance from the benab, and after this was done, he told the brothers, "Aim your arrow at the line and shoot."

In succession, the bothers, now with clean arrows, shot their arrows which struck the thin fishing line.

"Thank you, Adaba," the youngest brother said. "You have really taught us something new today and we will forever be grateful to you."

But Adaba had not yet completed his instructions in hunting.

"There is another important trick in shooting," he explained to them. "When you are hunting an animal, instead of aiming directly at an animal, point your arrow upward, so that it will descend and stick into the animal's back."

With Adaba's much needed help, the brothers practiced this method, and soon became very skilled hunters and from that day onward hardly missed when they shot at their prey.

And when Adaba decided to ask for their sister's hand in marriage, they did object in any way but readily agreed to have him as their brother-in-law. They took him back to their village and he and Simi lived very happily, and from time to time he joined the brothers in their hunting trips.

Then one day, Simi said to him, "Adaba, let's go for a walk near the river."

Adaba readily agreed, and when they arrived at the riverbank, Simi shouted, "Let's take a bath in the river."

And with that, she plunged into the river and swam back and forth.

"Jump in, Adaba," she shouted as she splashed about in the water.

But Adaba shouted back, "No, I never bathe in rivers but only in the water-holes inside the hollow trees."

However, she did not take him seriously and playfully splashed some water on him as he stood on the riverbank. After doing so for three times, she leaped out of the river and rushed to pull him into the water. Upon seizing his arm, he was instantly transformed himself into a frog and he hopped away rapidly to the forest and climbed back into his hollow tree trunk.

With tears streaming down her face and in great sorrow, she slowly returned home.

Her brothers asked her, "Where is Adaba?"

"He has left me and gone away," she wept.

"You must have done something really bad for him to leave you," her eldest brother berated her.

The other brothers fully agreed with this admonishment and shouted insults at her for not being good to their brother-in-law. But these insults only caused her to hurt more and to weep even more bitterly.

As for Adaba, he remained a frog in the hollow tree and never climbed out again in human form. And ever since the day he returned to his old home, the three brothers were no longer very successful in their hunting trips as when Adaba went with them.

Amerindian woman sitting in a hammock

~ 45 ~

The Woman Who Fought Two Tigers

A young woman who had gone to a far-off village set out one morning to return to her own home. To do so, she had to walk along some narrow paths through the forest in which many fierce animals lived. So, to protect herself, she carried a long sharp knife with which she hoped to defend herself.

After walking and resting intermittently for many hours, night approached, so she had to find a place to sleep. But with so many dangerous animals in the forest, she was worried that she could be attacked. She therefore decided to make a secure sleeping place among the branches of a young *eetay* palm. To make her sleeping place safe, she cut some thorny bushes and placed them around the base of the tree trunk. Having assured herself that the thorns would deter any wild animal from approaching her, she climbed onto the tree, which had three bunches of fruit hanging down from among its branches. As a further means of protection, she cut the stalk of each bunch (but not all the way through), thus allowing it to continue hanging so that any little disturbance would make it fall. She then nestled among the branches and, soon after, fell fast asleep.

Around midnight, she was awakened by the loud roaring of a tiger. The tiger had picked up her scent and was standing just below the eetay palm. He leaped at the trunk, but the thorn bushes pricked him and he yelped in pain as he backed away. But he was determined to get at the girl. So he sprang over the thorn bushes and wrapped his legs around the tree trunk and began to climb.

Meanwhile, the girl was terrified at the presence of the beast so near to her, but she was still determined to defend herself. She held her knife firmly, aiming to stab the tiger as soon as he got near.

Suddenly, the tiger grabbed at a bunch of eetay nuts in an attempt to pull himself among the branches. As he did so, the half-cut stem broke off; and the tiger, along with the bunch of nuts, crashed to the ground. However, this did not deter the beast, for he leaped on the tree once again and, in a second attempt to climb into the branches, he grabbed at another bunch of nuts. And as before, the half-cut stem snapped off, and he tumbled heavily to the ground again.

For a while, everything was quiet, and the young woman heard no other movement from the tiger. She peeped through the branches, and in the dim light, she saw him stretched out on his back beneath the tree. But she felt that he was just pretending to be injured. So she kept a close eye on him for the remainder of the night. At the break of dawn, she noticed that the tiger was in the same position since he fell. Then she observed, too, that his tongue was hanging out and covered with swarming ants. It immediately dawned on her that the tiger was dead and, most likely, had broken his neck when he fell.

With a sigh of relief, she climbed down the tree and continued her long and lonely journey. After walking for about an hour, she heard sounds of an axe cutting a tree. She felt a sense of relief knowing that she was now near to people, so she moved quickly to the area of the chopping sounds.

Luckily for her, her keen sight saved her from falling for the tricks of another tiger. This second tiger had seen her in the distance and decided to play an old trick to trap her. What he did was to hang from a tree branch by his front paws and lash the trunk with his tail, so as to produce the sound of a chopping axe. From time to time, he would also pull broken branches and throw them noisily to the ground to give the impression that the tree had fallen. He was confident that the young woman would approach, thinking she was near to woodcutters, and then he would pounce on her.

Through the trees, the young woman observed the tiger as he performed his tricks. His back was turned to her, so he did not see her quietly approaching with her long sharp knife. In a flash, she chopped off his tail as he whipped it on the tree trunk.

With a great howl, the tiger, now thoroughly ashamed he had no tail, fell off the tree and rushed way deep into the forest to examine his wounds.

So the young woman continued her journey, and after a while, she again heard sounds of trees being cut. This time, she was extra careful on approaching the sounds, but was much relieved when she saw that the woodcutters were four men from her own village.

As they gathered around her, she related her adventures to them—how she had killed one tiger and chopped off the tail of another. But they would not believe her.

"No woman can ever do such things," they argued.

"Well, if you don't believe me, let me take you to the places where I did these things," she responded.

With that, the men shouldered their axes and followed her back along the trail. She showed them the severed tail under the tree and then took them to the eetay palm under which the dead tiger lay. It was only then they really believed that the young woman was capable of such heroic deeds.

The eetay palm

~ 46 ~

Nohi and the Ogress

Nohi, a popular hunter, and his younger brother lived in a village on the edge of the forest. From time to time, Nohi journeyed into the forest in search of bush-hogs and deer. One day, as he was on one of his hunting trips, he arrived at a shallow creek. There he climbed a tree on the bank and waited for the animals, which would come to that location to quench their thirst.

From his perch, he suddenly spotted a tall old woman walking slowly in the creek. As she walked, she put her hand into the water and pulled up two fishes. Then she quickly ate one and put the other in a quake hanging from her shoulder.

On her head, she wore a calabash bowl upside down like a cap, which she removed intermittently and tossed into the water. The calabash would spin round and round like a top, and then the woman would pick it up and place it back on her head.

By her actions, Nohi was convinced the old woman was an ogress so, not wanting to make his presence known, he made sure he remained hidden from her view behind the thick leaves of the tree.

The woman continued her actions and passed under the tree still catching two fishes at a time, eating one and placing the other in her quake. Nohi observed her until she finally disappeared around a bend in the creek. As soon as the woman was out of sight, he quickly descended from the tree and hurried to his home where he arrived late that night. There, he related to his younger brother the entire story of the old woman he saw that day.

"I would like to see this woman who can catch fish so easily and eat them uncooked as well," his brother pleaded. "Please take me to the creek so I can see her."

"No! I don't think I should take you there because you laugh at everything, and you might laugh at her," Nohi answered. "She will thus discover our presence and may do harm to us."

His brother again begged him to take him to the creek, and it was only when he solemnly promised not to laugh at the old woman that Nohi agreed.

Early the next morning, they both set out for the creek, and on arrival a few hours later, they climbed the same tree on which Nohi had hidden the day before. But the younger brother, being inquisitive, wanted to have a clear view of the creek, so he perched on a branch hanging directly over the water.

The two brothers sat very quietly and waited for the old ogress to appear. Then, in the distance, they saw her spinning her calabash as she waded in the creek and pulled out two fishes every time she plunged her hand in the water. In amazement, they watched as she devoured one fish and placed the other in the quake hanging on her shoulder.

After a while, she arrived under the branch where the younger brother was hiding. Suddenly, she spotted the younger brother's reflection and thought that he was actually hiding in the creek. So she snatched at the reflection and, after failing to pull him out, continued grabbing at it again and again. Her actions seemed very comical to the younger brother, and he could not stop himself from laughing.

Hearing the laughter, the old woman looked up and saw him on the branch above her head. She was furious, and she yelled at him, "Come down here right now!"

But he continued laughing and shouted back, "No! I will not."

"Oh! You will not!" the old woman exclaimed. "Let me show you how I will bring you down."

Mumbling a few unintelligible words, she swung her arms and, magically, a huge swarm of red fire ants rushed up the tree and began stinging him. He screamed in pain, and as he tried to brush the ants away, he lost his balance and fell into the creek. Very quickly, the old woman—who indeed was an ogress—pulled him up from the water and devoured him.

Up in the tree, Nohi began wailing in grief when he saw the end of his brother. The ogress saw him among the leaves and screamed, "Climb down the tree right now!"

But just as his ill-fated brother had done, he too refused to budge.

Again, the ogress wielded her magic powers, and the swarm of red ants rushed at him. Not wanting to receive the painful stings they would inflict, he clambered down, fearful that he also would suffer the same fate as his brother.

As soon as he hit the ground, he attempted to run away, but the ogress grabbed him, and after magically reducing his size, she locked him away in her quake and took him to her home. There she removed the fishes from her quake, which she placed in a corner and covered with a heap of leaves.

Now the ogress had two daughters, Myra and Kura, and they watched in wonder as their mother heaped leaves on the quake. She turned to them and sternly instructed, "I am going to reap some cassava, and under no circumstance must you touch this quake while I am away."

But as soon as their mother departed, the girls, being curious as ever, wanted to know what was inside the quake.

"Why does Mother order us not to touch the quake?" Myra, the elder sister, asked.

"Maybe, she has something inside that she doesn't want us to see," Kura suggested. "I think we should open it see for ourselves."

So they quickly removed the leaves, and upon opening the quake, they saw the miniature Nohi inside. As soon as the younger sister took him out, the spell was removed and he at once reverted to his regular size.

"Who are you?" asked Myra.

"I am Nohi," he replied. "You mother captured me after she killed my brother."

"We are sorry she did that to you," Kura said.

The girls had a good look at him, and then Kura whispered to her sister, "What a nice young man is he!"

She instantly developed a great liking for him.

"Are you a good hunter and fisherman?" she asked.

"Yes," he responded. "If you save me from your mother, I can do a lot of hunting for all of you."

Kura thereupon hid him in her hammock, heaped the leaves again over the quake, and waited for their mother's return. Soon after, she came in with a bundle of cassava, and she began peeling and then cutting them into small pieces for the meal she planned. Definitely, she had intentions of eating Nohi as part of her meal. So, shortly after, she went to the quake to remove him. But she was astonished to find it empty.

"Where is the young man I had inside this quake?" she yelled at her daughters.

"We set him free, and I have him wrapped up in my hammock," Kura admitted. "But you cannot kill him because I want him as my husband because he is a good hunter."

The ogress's temper abated, and she mumbled resignedly, "All right! You can have him as your husband as long as he brings fish for me to eat.

But I want you to know that the first day he comes home with nothing, I will eat him for my dinner."

Starting the very next day, Nohi went to sea regularly to catch fish for her. But no matter what quantity of fish he brought back, the old ogress would eat all—except three, which the two sisters and Nohi would cook for their dinner.

However, after many weeks had passed, Nohi became tired of the tedious task of catching so many fish for the ogress.

"Your mother will use me as her slave for the rest of my life to get fish for her," he complained to his wife one evening. "I have to escape from this place to be free of her."

Kura sympathized with him, and they began to make plans for the two of them to escape. Eventually, Nohi came up with an idea. So on his last intended trip to the sea, using a rope tied to a heavy piece of rock, he anchored his *corial* (with the catch in it) a little farther out from the shore than he had done before. Here, the water was deeper, and he knew that dangerous sharks frequented that area of the sea. Making sure he did not see any, he swiftly swam ashore and rushed home.

"So, finally, you have come home without catching anything," his mother-in-law said.

"Don't think so for a moment," Nohi replied. "I made such a big catch that I want you to help me bring it home."

"And where is your catch?" she demanded.

"It's in my corial, anchored in the sea," Nohi explained.

The old woman, gleefully expecting a large quantity of fish, readily set out with Nohi to the seaside. She saw the corial floating in the water and, in great anticipation, she plunged into the sea and swam out to it. But as soon as she held on to the side of the corial, a huge shark lurking below leaped up, grabbed her in its fearsome jaws, and pulled her to the bottom of the sea.

Nohi, from the shore, witnessed all of this, and he knew that the ogress's hold over him had now disappeared forever. He hurried home, told his wife what had happened, and Nohi swiftly led her away from the area.

Meanwhile, Myra—who was in their nearby farm—saw Kura and Nohi hurriedly departing from the house. She immediately sensed that something was wrong when she noticed that her mother had not returned. Despite her mother being an ogress, she still loved her, and she was worried that Nohi was somehow responsible for her nonappearance. She ran all the way to the seaside, hoping to find her mother there, but failed to locate her anywhere along the beach.

As she continued her search, she came across some bloody pieces of her mother's clothes stuck to some driftwood. Her dismay of not finding her mother turned into rage. She was now convinced that Nohi had caused her death and that he was escaping with her sister.

In great anger, she hastened home, and after sharpening her cutlass, she set out to follow the trail of Nohi and her sister. After a while, she saw them in the distance and raced behind them on the savannah. As she came near, Nohi saw her expression of rage and her threatening actions with her cutlass.

"Run, Kura, run!" he yelled to his wife. "Your sister is coming to kill us!"

Without any hesitation, Kura raced away with Nohi following closely behind. The angry sister chased them and was getting dangerously close with her cutlass raised for a chopping blow just as Kura and Nohi reached a tall tree. Kura hurriedly climbed it with her husband close behind.

The enraged sister also clambered up behind them, but she was hampered since she had only one hand free.

Nohi pushed his wife forward and urged her, "Climb higher!"

In the meantime, his sister-in-law clambered behind him, but he leaped from branch to branch to escape her sharp cutlass. She managed to nick him in his leg, but that did not hamper his agility. But in the course of all the action, Myra lost the grip on her cutlass and it tumbled to the ground. In the ensuing confusion, Nohi and Kura managed to descend the tree, and they quickly made their escape to the nearby forest.

Nohi quickly led his wife through a series of trails he had used as a hunter, and after journeying for many hours, they reached his former home where he and his brother once lived. There they resided and never saw Myra again.

A quake

~ 47 ~

The Wrong Rattle

A man and his wife, with two teenage daughters and two younger sons, lived in a small village on the bank of a narrow creek. One day, the parents and their sons departed for the neighboring village to attend an overnight party, while the girls remained at home to make casiri.

As the girls walked along a path to fetch some water from the creek, they heard the screeching cry of a hawk emanating from the surrounding bushes. Little did they know that it was Siwara, a bush spirit—or hebu—and not a hawk that was making such a sound. He was at that time trying out his skills at imitating bird sounds.

This screeching sound continued as the girls returned from the creek, and it became so annoying that the elder girl threw a stick into the bushes and shouted, "Stop that foolish noise and show yourself!"

Immediately the screeching stopped, but the girl noticed that the hawk—which they thought was the noisemaker—did not fly away as they walked back to their home to continue their chores.

While they were busy making casiri, a young man approached the house.

"Good day," he greeted them. "My name is Siwara. Where are your parents?"

"They are at a party in the next village," the younger sister replied.

Unaware that the stranger was no other than the hebu Siwara who had changed himself into human form, the girls took an instant liking for him, for he was quite pleasant and mannerly. They even offered him a meal of delicious boiled cassava, which he consumed wholeheartedly.

"Thank you very much for the meal," the young man said. "I will leave now, but I will return with a large powis I shot today. You can cook its meat for dinner."

He soon departed, and within an hour, he was back with the powis as promised. He also brought his folded hammock draped across his shoulders.

"Will you allow me to stay here tonight?" he requested. "I can sleep under the benab outside."

The girls readily agreed and helped Siwara hang his hammock under the benab at the side of the house. Later, the young man even helped the girls roast the powis meat for their dinner, and after a hearty meal, they all climbed into their own hammocks and fell fast asleep.

Just after daybreak, Siwara told the girls, "I am leaving now to go into the forest, but please do not tell your parents that I was here."

The girls promised not to reveal that information as he waved good-bye to them.

Later that morning, their parents and brothers returned home from the party. Their mother immediately saw some of the leftover roasted powis meat and inquired, "Where did you get this powis meat?"

The sisters did not want to reveal how they acquired the meat since they had promised Siwara not to reveal any information about him.

"A hawk killed the powis," the elder sister explained. "We chased away the hawk and brought the powis home."

Meanwhile, their father could not resist having a taste, so he tore off a piece of the meat. And as he chewed it, he bit a fragment of a kookrit arrow embedded in it. Turning to his daughters, he questioned, "If a hawk killed this powis, how did this kookrit arrow hit it?"

The sisters looked at each other, now fully aware that they could no longer lie about how they obtained the powis.

"I'm sorry we didn't tell you the truth, Father," the younger daughter admitted. "A young man named Siwara brought it to us yesterday, and he slept under the benab last night."

With an angry frown on his face, the father asked, "And where is that young man?"

"He left early this morning for the forest," replied the younger girl.

"Why didn't you tell me this in the first place?" he admonished them, still greatly annoyed. "Go right now and call out for him."

Somewhat relieved to get away from the presence of their angry father, the two girls hurried into the bushes near the creek and began shouting, "Siwara! Siwara!"

From among the bushes, Siwara, who was there in his spirit form, shouted back, "I am here."

"Our father wants to meet you," the elder sister shouted again.

Suddenly, Siwara emerged from the bushes in human form, and he followed the girls back to their house. There, the girls introduced him to their parents and brothers, and they were all quickly taken in with his charm and good manners.

Their father—who was still somewhat intoxicated with the amount of paiwarri he had consumed at the party the night before—was very talkative, and he chatted away and laughed uproariously at Siwara's jokes. Of course, he, like the rest of his family, did not know that the young man was really a hebu in disguise. He soon developed a great liking for Siwara and felt that he would make a good husband for his elder daughter.

"My elder daughter is of marriageable age," he told Siwara. "I would be very happy if you are married to her."

It so happened that Siwara already felt a great attraction for the girl, and he readily agreed to the proposal. A few days after, the marriage took place, and Siwara moved in to live with the family.

The young man proved to be a good provider and was always successful whenever he went into the forest to hunt. He also decided to teach his brothers-in-law how to hunt for bush-hogs. The boys, who already had some skills in using their bows and arrows, had never seen bush-hogs before, so it was a great opportunity for them when Siwara took them on one of his hunting trips in the forest to show them how to hunt for these wild animals.

On arriving at a particular area in the forest, he unhooked a rattle hanging from his belt and shook it loudly. Suddenly, a group of bush-hogs rushed in as if they were obeying the sound.

"These are the bush-hogs," shouted Siwara. "Shoot them now!"

But the two brothers, in sheer fright, scaled a tree to get out of the way of the fierce animals. Siwara had to shoot three of the animals himself, which they eventually carried back home.

In the days that followed, he took the brothers on more hunting trips, and they soon overcame their fear of bush-hogs and were able to successfully shoot a few of them.

From time to time, Siwara brought some of his possessions from the forest to his parents-in-law's home. Among these were four rattles used only for hunting bush-hogs. He explained to the family that there were two kinds of bush-hogs, the timid and the very savage, and he had a pair of rattles for each kind—one to call the animals, and the other to chase them away.

He then gave a stern warning to the entire household: "On no account must any of you touch these rattles when I am not here. Because if you do, it will bring trouble."

Not long after that stern warning, trouble indeed came. Siwara had gone to his father-in-law's farm, and his younger brother-in-law who had remained at home saw the beautiful rattles, all adorned with feathers, hanging in a row on the wall. He took one down, examined it carefully, and—apparently forgetting what Siwara had ordered—shook it loudly.

Immediately, a loud screeching sound emanated from the nearby forest. That particular rattle was the one to summon the wild bush-hogs, all of which raced through the bushes into the village. The villagers were terrified and had to hurriedly escape by mounting trees or climbing to their rooftops to escape from them.

As the fierce bush-hogs rampaged through the village and destroyed everything in their path, Sirawa heard the screams of the people as they called for him to help chase away the beasts. In great haste, he raced to the house where he shook the proper rattle, and the bush-hogs quickly disappeared back into the forest.

Obviously, Sirawa was extremely angry.

"You disobeyed my instructions," he yelled at his brother-in-law. "I cannot trust you near my possessions anymore."

So that very day he gathered all his possessions, including his hunting rattles, and left with his wife for his forest home. No one ever saw them again.

Amerindian rattles

~ 48 ~

The Hunter and the Tigress

Yeno, a young man, was a very skilled hunter. He was particularly adept at hunting bush-hogs, and every time he went on a hunting trip, he would kill at least five or six of these animals.

Because of his great success at hunting, a tigress followed his tracks leading to where the bush-hogs lived, and she would eventually succeed in killing one or two for herself after the hunter departed with those that he shot.

Now this tigress was a very unique animal since she had lived among the hebus and had inevitably learned to apply magic to change herself into human form whenever she wanted. So one day, in the form of a beautiful young woman, she waited for Yeno as he walked along a forest trail. He was struck by her beauty and immediately became enamored with her.

"My name is Reya, and I've watched you hunting in the forest," she told him. "How do you manage to kill so many bush-hogs?"

Upon hearing these words from such a beautiful young woman, Yeno felt really proud of himself.

"I've been hunting for these animals since I was a little boy," he explained. "My father trained me in all these hunting skills."

"I myself have been hunting these animals for a long time," the young woman stated. "But I would like to learn some of your skills."

"Well, you can meet me when I come to hunt, and I will show you some of the tricks I use," he told her. He was certainly excited that this charming young woman wanted to be in his company. But she was not content with that answer from Yeno.

"You are indeed a handsome young man, and I've admired you for a long time," she said. "How about if I become your wife? Then we can hunt bush-hogs together."

Yeno was dumbstruck, for he himself was secretly hoping for such an arrangement.

"Yes! Yes! That is something I'll certainly like," he quickly agreed.

But the young woman added, "Before we get married though, you must agree to one condition—that you live with me in my home deep in the forest and not return to your own village."

And without giving it a second thought, for he felt so deeply in love with her, Yeno eagerly consented to this proposal.

"But there is one more important thing you should know," she stated. "I am really a tigress who lived with the hebus, and through the magic I learned, I changed myself into a woman."

Yeno was thunderstruck on hearing this admission.

"That is difficult for me to believe," he told her. "You are a woman, and there is nothing in you that would make me believe you were a tigress."

"Well, I'm a woman now, but if you ever allow my secret to be publicly exposed, I will change back into a tigress and you will never see me again," she explained to him.

He promised faithfully that he would never reveal her secret, and later that day, she took him to her home deep into the forest. There they lived happily together as husband and wife, and she never changed back to her animal form. She also proved to be an excellent cook, and soon, with his training, became very skilled at hunting bush-hogs as well.

Now although Yeno lived with his wife for such a long time, he never revealed much about himself or his family. One day, she finally asked him, "Are your parents still alive? Do you have brothers and sisters?"

"Yes. My parents are alive, and I have brothers and sisters," he answered.

"Well, they haven't seen you for a long time," she declared. "Why don't we go and visit them?"

"All right," he agreed readily. "But before we go, we should hunt some bush-hogs and take the meat for them."

After their hunting trip, she led Yeno along a series of pathways that took him to a familiar part of the forest. From that point, he took the lead, and soon after, they arrived at his parents' home on the forest's edge.

The entire family was overjoyed to see him, for in his long absence, everyone thought he had died in some unknown location in the forest. As was expected, all his relatives admired his wife, and his old mother asked, "Where did you get such a beautiful wife?"

"We met one day in the forest while I was hunting," he replied.

But he was especially careful not to divulge too much information since he did not want anyone to ever know that his wife was originally a tigress.

"And where have you been living all this time?" his mother probed.

"My wife has a house deep in the forest," he explained. "We have been living there since we first met."

For those few days that Yeno and his wife lived at his parents' home, his relatives, from time to time, questioned Reya about her family background. But she offered as little information as possible, only revealing that she came from a family living far away in the forest.

After a week had passed, the couple went on a hunt for bush-hogs and later returned with a large bag of meat. All the villagers knew of Yeno's ability to hunt, but when they saw the unusually large quantity of bush-hog meat the two brought, they were sure that his wife also had extraordinary hunting abilities.

So all the villagers, as his relatives had done before, began to question Yeno and his wife about the latter's family background. As before, they again repeated that she belonged to a family living deep in the forest. But that did not ease their suspicion that the beautiful young woman had some sort of a mystery surrounding her.

Of all the others, Yeno's mother was more insistent in asking questions about her daughter-in-law. She kept pressing her son for more details, but he never revealed anything more since he was determined to keep his promise not to reveal any information about his wife's real origin.

But his mother continued to pester him, and one afternoon while they were alone, she continued her pleading.

"Please tell me more about Reya's family background," she implored. "I am an old woman, and I will not rest in my grave if you don't tell me more."

And since he loved his mother very much, he finally revealed Reya's secret to her and warned her not to ever let anyone else know about it.

"I will keep this secret in my heart and will carry it to my grave," she assured her son.

But one evening, at the house next door to hers, the old woman was at a casiri party with some other women neighbors, and they pressed her for more information about her mysterious daughter-in-law. She repeated to them what they had already heard, that Reya's relatives lived far away and deep in the forest. But they were not satisfied with that answer, so they willfully gave her more and more casiri to drink and threw question after question to her about her daughter-in-law. Finally, the old woman, now fully intoxicated, could no longer hold the secret.

She shouted out, "Reya is really a tigress who changed herself to a woman!"

Instantly, as the secret was exposed, Reya—who was chatting with her husband in his parents' house—at once transformed back into a tigress. With a loud and powerful roar, she raced away back into the forest.

Poor brokenhearted Yeno ran behind her, shouting her name all the way, but he never ever saw her again.

An Amerindian family

~ 49 ~

The Manatee and the Porpoise

Two sisters found a friendly tapir, Maipuri, in the forest; and he soon learned to obey whenever they called for him. Maipuri was a clever tapir indeed. Whenever the sisters went in search of wild fruits, he would lead them to the plum trees in the forest, for he knew exactly where they were located.

Maipuri himself loved plum juice, and so he eagerly accompanied the sisters since he knew they would give him some of the delicious beverage to drink. After returning from the forest, they would squeeze the juice from the plums and then signal Maipuri by whistling through their fingers for him to come and get his share of the juice.

Very soon, Maipuri became their big pet, and he accompanied them everywhere they went in the forest. Because of his size and strength, he also acted as their protector and deterred any dangerous animal from attacking them.

But the girls' brother soon became jealous over the attention they paid to Maipuri. So one day, he secretly followed them as they traversed the forest in search of ripe plums, and he was able to detect the places that the tapir frequented when he was not with the girls.

As the girls went out one afternoon to reap cassava on their farm, their brother slipped away into the forest and hurried to an area where the plum trees were laden with ripe fruit. He knew this was a location near to where Maipuri lived.

While waiting there, he placed his fingers to his lips and whistled as his sisters did when they summoned Maipuri; and in no time, the unsuspecting tapir rushed through the bushes to the location of the call. As Maipuri approached, the cruel young man shot him through the heart with his bow and arrow, killing him instantly. He then methodically cut up the animal's body into little pieces, which he scattered in various parts of the forest.

The following morning, the girls, deciding to make some more plum-drink, set out for the same clump of plum trees near to where their brother had carried out his ugly deed. As usual, they whistled for Maipuri, but he did not appear. They whistled again and again, but there was no sign of the tapir.

The girls all at once felt that something tragic had happened to Maipuri, so they began a search of the surrounding area. It was then that they discovered the place where he was butchered, and they found bloody pieces of his remains scattered on the ground.

Wailing loudly, they grieved for Maipuri and wondered who could have been so cruel as to slaughter their friend. They continued to weep as they arrived on the bank of a river, and in great distress, the older sister jumped into the river, hoping to end her life. The younger sister screamed from the riverbank and plunged after her sister, hoping to rescue her, but because she also could not swim, she sank rapidly to the riverbed.

As all of this was going on, a water spirit who lived in the river depths observed their struggles in the water and, having pity for them, instantly changed the older sister into a powerful manatee and transformed the younger sister into a graceful porpoise.

The manatee

~ 50 ~

Amalivaca

Long ago, shortly after the end of the first great flood, Amalivaca—a young man wearing a majestic, beautiful headdress—paddled his canoe up the Essequibo River. His journey was indeed long and tedious, for he came from a land far across the seas. Not long after he arrived, he thought of building his home on the land near this awesome river, but then he also thought of traveling over this new land first before deciding where to finally settle.

Although the waters had drained from the land, the rivers were still heavily flooded—so much so that their waters reached far up the valley sides. As Amalivaca paddled his canoe up the rivers, he thought it wise to mark his path. So he used a large diamond to scratch huge drawings of people, animals, and strange shapes on the rock walls at different points along the rivers. He also made drawings on many outcrops of rock that stuck up in the middle of the rivers.

Later, as the water level subsided, Amalivaca's drawings remained on the rocks, high above the river level. As time passed, the Amerindians called these drawings *timehri*, or rock drawings. Even to this day, they can still be seen on the upper courses of the many rivers in Guyana.

One day as he continued his many travels, Amalivaca arrived at an Amerindian village on the bank of the Cuyuni River. He immediately noticed some men planting sticks on a patch of ground.

"What are you planting?" Amalivaca inquired.

"We're planting arrow cane reeds. We'll use them to make good arrows," one man replied.

"But why do you need so many arrows?"

"We need them to either make war against others or to defend ourselves," another man told him.

Upon hearing this last answer, Amalivaca became very angry. "Why should you make war against other people?" he asked. "Don't you see you're wasting your time? Rather than planting arrow cane reeds for arrows, why don't you cultivate cassava, sweet potatoes, corn, and other fruits?"

On hearing this, the men stopped planting and crowded around Amalivaca who tied up his canoe and stood on the riverbank.

"You seem to have sensible thoughts, stranger," a man said. "Why don't you stay with us and show us how to cultivate more crops?"

By this time, some of the men began admiring Amalivaca's canoe.

"How is it that your canoe is so well-shaped and smooth inside?" a young man asked. "We use axes to hollow our canoes, but they are not so nicely and beautifully shaped as yours."

"I used fire to hollow mine," Amalivaca replied. "If you're willing to learn, I'll teach you how."

Anxious to share his many ideas with the villagers, he stayed on for a few months. During this time, he taught the people to cultivate food crops effectively and use fire to hollow canoes.

Finally, he was ready to continue his travels; but before doing so, he gave some sound advice to the people.

"You have new knowledge now," he told them. "But knowledge isn't to be locked up. You must share it with others, so they too can learn the good things you already know."

The people obeyed him. Soon, the skills Amalivaca taught were known to all the people in the region.

After Amalivaca left that village, he visited many others in various parts of the country, teaching and assisting people. By this time, he was so well-known that his fame preceded him. He had also displayed the magical powers he possessed to assist some villages. All over, people eagerly looked forward to seeing and meeting with him.

At a small village in the Mazaruni River area, the residents tested Amalivaca.

"Amalivaca, we use the river a lot to travel," they told him. "It's very difficult to paddle our canoes against the current. Please use your magical powers to make the river flow downriver on one side and upriver on the other. That will certainly make it easy for us to paddle in any direction."

Always eager to please people, Amalivaca tried to comply; but despite how much magic he used, he failed to make the current flow upstream.

"This may be because too much rain falls in the Pakaraima Mountains," he reasoned. "The steady rain fills the rivers, and the water constantly rushes to the sea."

Still, he was determined to show the people some result, or they would lose faith in him. "I am going to the great wide sea for a while," he told them. "When I return, there will be a two-way flow of the current."

Upon his arrival at sea, just off the mouth of the Essequibo River, he used his magic to create the tides. His magic caused the water of the sea to rush up the rivers for a great distance during high tide. This made at least part of the river flow upstream. At low tide, the current flowed downstream as usual.

When he returned to the village, the people were pleased. "The current goes upriver part of the day," they said. "That is very helpful."

Shortly after, Amalivaca journeyed through the Corentyne, Potaro, Siparuni, and Rupununi Rivers, spreading knowledge everywhere. Eventually, he came to the plains of Maita where he made his home in a large cave. There he relaxed by playing soothing music on instruments that he made.

Just outside his cave, he also hollowed out a large rock, which he used as a drum to make music. To this day, the hollow rock still stands outside the cave on the Maita plains, and Amerindians in that area refer to it as the Drum of Amalivaca.

Many people went to Amalivaca's home on the plains to meet him and seek knowledge. He taught them to use herbs to cure sickness and showed them how to use the stars to guide them when they traveled at night.

As time passed and Amalivaca grew older, he was pleased that the people had learned all he wanted them to know.

"My mission in this land is over," he told them. "It's time for me to leave you."

Then early one morning, the old gray-haired Amalivaca prepared to take his leave. As he was about to set out in his canoe, a group of people gathered on the bank of the river to bid him farewell. They all stood in silence, sadness written all over their faces as they watched as he paddled away into the distance. With one final wave, Amalivaca steered his canoe around a bend of the river and disappeared from sight.

The people in that land saw him no more. But Amalivaca—after leaving the mighty Essequibo River—entered the wide Atlantic Ocean where he sailed about, hoping to meet and share his knowledge with other groups of people.

Rock outcrop with pictographs

Rock with *timehri* drawing

Rock drawings in Essequibo River

GLOSSARY

acouri—This large rodent is also known as the agouti.

awarra—A common palm (*Astrocaryum vulgare*) found near to Amerindian villages in the forested hinterland. It bears bunches of small yellow fruits when ripe, and these are eaten with great relish. Each fruit has a round seed, the kernel of which can be used for making oil.

balata—A form of natural rubber formed from the sap of the bulletwood tree (*Mimusops globosa*).

balata bleeders—Men who tap the bulletwood tree for its sap.

benab—A small tentlike shelter made of palm leaves and sticks. It is often constructed by Amerindians when they are on long fishing and hunting expeditions.

black tiger—The South American black puma.

calabash—A large green gourd; the fruit of the calabash tree. The outer skin of the gourd becomes hard as it ages. When it is cut into two equal parts and the inner white pith is removed, two strong bowls are produced. Each of these bowls is also called a calabash.

camudi—A large snake that measures a maximum of eight meters in length and one meter in circumference at its thickest part. There are two types of camudi—the land camudi, known as the *boa constrictor*, and the water camudi, which frequents swamps and rivers.

casareep (pronounced *kyaz-rip*)—A thick treaclelike liquid obtained after the juice of the bitter cassava is boiled for a long time. It can be stored for long periods and is used for the preparation of the famous Guyanese dish, pepperpot.

casiri—A pleasant-tasting pink alcoholic drink made from sweet potatoes and sugarcane. Sometimes, a small amount of cassava is added. It is prepared by boiling the ingredients and leaving them to ferment.

cassava—The elongated tuberous root of the cassava or manioc plant.

cassava bread—When the juice from the grated cassava is removed, the dry cassava meal is broken in a sieve. After it is sifted, it becomes a coarse flour. Some of this moistened flour is flattened in a round shape and placed on a circular stone, or a circular flat piece of iron over a fire, where it is baked. This is the cassava bread. After both sides are baked, the cassava bread is thrown on the thatched roof of the house to dry in the sun. Once dried, it keeps for weeks.

corial—A dug-out canoe.

crabwood—A big tree that grows to over twenty-five meters in height. Its timber produces a very strong, dark brown wood. The tree bears a nut from which an unpleasant-smelling oil known as crab-oil is extracted.

curare—A poison extracted from the bark of a creeping plant known as *urari*. The Amerindians call the poison *ourali*. This poison is smeared onto arrowheads and darts for blowpipes. If the poison is smeared on an arrow that is kept warm and dry, it can retain its effectiveness for several years.

cutlass—Before iron and steel implements became known to the Amerindians, the cutlass was made of stone. As with the modern implement, it was a slightly curved sword, with only one edge being sharp.

eetay (or ite)—This is the *Mauritia flexuosa* palm that grows in large stands in the Guyana forest. It is of immense economic value to the Amerindians.

farine—Cassava-meal with the juice removed is dried on a flat circular stone or iron on a slow fire. It is not allowed to stick together and, after a while, it resembles dry brown crumbs. These crumbs are known as farine, which forms an important ingredient in Amerindian meals.

haiarri—A small plant, the roots of which produce narcotic juices. Amerindians fish by placing pieces of the roots, which are first crushed, in small streams near to a temporary dam. Fish are rendered unconscious by the juices from the roots.

harpy eagle—The largest eagle in the world. It is now very rare and is regarded as endangered. Its natural habitat is the Pakaraima and Kanuku Mountains of Guyana.

hebus—A type of mischief-making forest spirit. Some are noted for their kindness to humans.

heron—A medium-sized bird found in swampy areas along the banks of rivers. Most of them are white in color; but there are some that are red, pink, blue, or gray. The gray heron is slightly smaller than the other species.

hima-heru—A small plant that grows in the interior of Guyana. It is claimed that when two pieces of its dry branches are rubbed together, they catch afire very quickly.

howling monkey—This large monkey (*Mycetes seniculus*) lives in the forest and howls very loudly. It is colloquially referred to as a "baboon" even though there are no real baboons in Guyana.

iguana—A large green lizard that lives among the branches of trees. It is hunted for its flesh which, when cooked, is regarded as a delicacy to its consumers.

imiri—A tiny river fish (*Sciadeicthys*).

jacamar—This is a small-to-medium-sized perching bird with a long bill and tail. It frequents low-altitude woodlands and forests.7

kiskadee—A small yellow-and-black bird with a band of white feathers around its head.

kookrit—This is the *Maximiliana regia* palm tree that abounds in the interior of Guyana. The ripe outer flesh of its fruit is very tasty. The kernel of the seed is used to make oil.

labba—This animal of the rodent family, also known as *paca*, is hunted for its savory meat.

lau-lau—This is a very large river fish (*Silurus*) of the catfish family. It sometimes weighs more than three hundred pounds (about one hundred and thirty-seven kilograms).

lukanani—A fish (*Cichla ocellaris*) that lives in the smaller rivers of Guyana. It attains a length of about one meter when fully grown.

manicole—The tall *Euterpe oleracea* palm that grows in the interior of Guyana.

matapee—A pliable basketwork cylinder used by Amerindians for squeezing out the juice from the grated cassava. It is about two meters long and fifteen centimeters in diameter.

mora—A giant hardwood forest tree (*Mora gonggrijpii*).

morocut—A food fish somewhat like the pacu (*Myletes*).

paddy (also *padi*)—The husk-covered unmilled rice grain.

paiwarri—An alcoholic drink that is most popular among Amerindians. It is made from thick cassava bread that is specially baked until it is dark brown. This is then broken into little pieces and placed in a large pot filled with water. When the pot is filled, it is stirred. After a period of slight boiling, the contents are left to ferment for a few days. Sometimes, sugarcane juice is added. The result is a brown alcoholic drink.

pegall—A basketlike container, either rectangular or round, with a cover that is of the same shape as the bottom or basket section. It is used for keeping personal items such as clothing.

pepperpot—A most popular dish made by boiling meat or fish with hot pepper and casareep.

piaman—An Amerindian "medicine man." He acts as doctor, fortune-teller, rainmaker, spellbinder, and dream interpreter. He is also a teacher, preacher, and counselor. He is generally highly respected.

powis—Also known as the *curassow*, this bird lives in the forest. It is as large as a turkey and is generally black in color with yellow beak and legs. It is hunted for its meat.

quake—A round basketlike container used by fishermen to keep their catch.

tapir—A medium-sized animal that lives in the forests of Guyana. It has very thick skin and a long snout and somewhat resembles a large pig. It is also known as *kama*, *maipuri*, bush cow, or bush donkey.

tiger—All large members of the cat family that live in Guyana's forests are called "tigers" by the local people, even though no tiger actually exists in the country. The smaller species, ocelots, are often referred to as "tiger cats." Generally, what is called a tiger is the large spotted jaguar.

timber grants—Areas in the forests where timber is cut commercially.

timehri—An Amerindian word that refers to the drawings and engravings found on rocks, especially near waterfalls, on the rivers in Guyana's interior.

troolie—The *Manicaria* palm, the leaves of which are used for thatch.

trumpet bird—This bird is also known as the *warracaba*. It is light gray in color, with deep purple-black feathers on its throat and neck. It utters a deep sound similar to that of a trumpet.

vaqueros—Cowboys who work on the cattle ranches of the Rupununi savannahs.

warrampa—A basketlike cover.

water-dog—The Guyanese name for an otter.

yawarri—This is the Guyanese name for the opossum, which is also known as *manicou* and *maracou*.

FURTHER READING

1. Armellada, Cesaréo de, *Tauron Pantón. Cuentos y Leyendas de Los Indios Pemón,* Ministerio de Educación, Caracas, 1964.
2. Brett, William H. *The Indian Tribes of Guiana.* (1882). im Thurn, Everard F., *Among the Indians of Guiana.* (1883); republished by Dover Publications Inc., New York, 1967.
3. Lambert, Leonard, *Guiana Legends,* Roffey and Clark, London, 1931.
4. Manuela de Cora, Maria, (ed.), *Kuai-Mare: Mitos Aborígenes de Venezuela*, Oceanida, Madrid, 1957.
5. Perrin, Michel, *The Way of the Dead Indians: Guajiro Myths and Symbols*, University of Texas Press, 1987.
6. Roth, Walter E., *An Inquiry into the Animism and Folklore of the Guiana Indians,* [from the Thirtieth Annual Report of the Bureau of American Ethnology, 1908-1909], Washington DC, 1915.

THE AUTHOR

D r. Odeen Ishmael, a veteran Guyanese diplomat, is currently Ambassador of Guyana to the State of Kuwait. Before his current appointment in January 2011, he served for seven years as Ambassador to Venezuela and, before that, from 1993 to 2003 as his country's Ambassador to the United States and concurrently in that period as Permanent Representative to the Organization of American States (OAS). He had the distinction of serving as Chairman of the Permanent Council of the OAS for two periods—in 1994 and 2003—the only diplomat from the Caribbean region to do so twice.

Up to 2003, he also represented Guyana at the United Nations and at other international forums such as the Organization of the Islamic Conference (OIC), and during 2003-2010 at forums of the Union of South American Nations (UNASUR) and the Latin America and Caribbean Economic System (SELA). He served as Chairman of SELA, headquartered in Venezuela, during 2009-2010.

In his early career, the author worked as a teacher for almost three decades, both in Guyana and the Commonwealth of the Bahamas. Since the 1970s, he has been a premier writer on the problems and perspectives of education in Guyana and the wider Caribbean region. He continues to write extensively on Guyanese history and culture and political developments in the Caribbean and Latin America. His writings on these subjects are published in newspapers and journals in Guyana, the wider Caribbean, North America, and the Latin American region.

His published books include *The Democracy Perspective in the Americas, Problems of the Transition of Education in the Third World, Towards Education Reform in Guyana, Amerindian Legends of Guyana*, and *The Magic Pot—Nansi Stories From The Caribbean*.

An Internet edition of his documentary history of the Guyana-Venezuela border controversy, *The Trail of Diplomacy*, was released in late 1998.

Further, he has compiled a lengthy collection of original documents on the Guyana-Venezuela border issue under the title *Guyana's Western Border*, also published on the Internet which also carries an online edition of his history of Guyana, *The Guyana Story*. In addition, as editor of the online GNI Publications, he has published a series of documents on Guyanese history.

For his work in diplomacy, the author received one of Guyana's highest honors—the Cacique Crown of Honour—in May 1997. And during his stint in the United States, he received the prestigious King Legacy Award for International Service from the International Committee to Commemorate the Life and Legacy of Martin Luther King Jr. in January 2002. Significantly, the US Congress paid a special tribute to him by a joint resolution in October 2003 just before he completed his service in the United States.

He and his wife Evangeline have two children.